"By Jove, 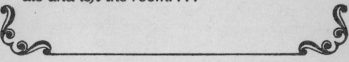 rium-
phantly as

He wheel room
while Lady nent.
He placed t able,
climbed up bed, and enfolded Lady
Harriet in his arms. She was a strong
woman and fought fiercely to break free
when he first began to kiss her. Whether her
abject surrender was caused by a realization of the futility of the struggle or from
other causes entirely remained forever a
moot question in Lady Harriet's mind.

"If you were trying to make me jealous,"
the colonel quoted, "it worked a fair treat,
lass." Well satisfied with this line's effect
upon his audience, he then retrieved his candle and left the room. . . .

Also by Marian Devon
*Published by Fawcett Books:*

MISS ARMSTEAD WEARS BLACK GLOVES
MISS ROMNEY FLIES TOO HIGH
M'LADY RIDES FOR A FALL
SCANDAL BROTH
ESCAPADE
FORTUNES OF THE HEART
THE HEATHER AND THE BLADE
GEORGIANA
A QUESTION OF CLASS
SIR SHAM
JADE

# LADY HARRIET TAKES CHARGE

## Marian Devon

FAWCETT CREST • NEW YORK

A Fawcett Crest Book
Published by Ballantine Books
Copyright © 1990 by Marian Pope Rettke

Library of Congress Catalog Card Number: 90-93288

ISBN 0-449-21738-8

Manufactured in the United States of America

First Edition: January 1991

# Chapter One

"You've asked *who* where?"

Lord Fawcett lowered the newspaper he'd been reading to gape at his young bride.

"Actually, shouldn't that be *whom*, sir?" Lady Fawcett, not far removed from the schoolroom, was still bothered by such distinctions.

"Who—whom—what the devil difference does that make? If my ears didn't deceive me, *disaster*'s the word we're looking for."

The couple was alone in the drawing room of Fairoaks Hall. Lord Fawcett, sprawled in his favorite wing chair, his evening pumps resting on a cross-framed stool, was catching up on the news. Before his bride had dropped her bombshell, he'd been following the progress of an international congress currently taking place in Vienna, in an attempt to put together a new map of Europe now that the monster Bonaparte had abdicated. On the other side of a bronze gilt standing lamp, Lady Fawcett perched on the edge of an armless, caned-seat chair and studiously frowned at her tambouring. To any casual observer they would have presented a cozy, domestic scene.

1

But there was nothing cozy about their situation. In the first place, Lady Fawcett found the gigantic drawing room with its ornate gilded ceiling, its black marble chimney pieces, its flocked crimson walls, its damask window hangings, and its gold satin carpet far too grand for comfort. Her parents had tried to impress upon her the enormity of the matrimonial prize she had captured, but they'd not prepared her sufficiently for the opulence and magnitude of Fairoaks. She was prone to recall with misty-eyed nostalgia the intimate honeymoon suite they'd shared in Venice a short month—or a lifetime—ago.

Still, she might have been able to cope with this sudden elevation had it not been for the atmosphere created by Lord Fawcett's daughter and her closest friend. Upon their arrival at the Hall the week before, Lady Selina had set the tone for the treatment of the second Lady Fawcett, and her friend, Miss Susan Tunstall, had followed suit. In so far as it was possible, the twosome had ignored the bride's existence. This evening, for example, they had retired directly after dinner to Selina's bedchamber where they were indulging in a comfortable, and spiteful, coze. When Lord Fawcett had finished his solitary port, expecting to join all three young ladies, he had found his wife, industriously tambouring, and quite alone.

Lord Fawcett was not a sensitive man. He was slow to identify the true source of the unease he'd been feeling for several days. So it was now almost a relief to at last have something concrete to focus on.

"My God, Mariana," he frowned, "have you any notion of just what you've done?"

"Why no, sir." Her hand trembled and botched the embroidery she was determined to keep working on.

2

"And—I've mentioned this before—please don't call me 'sir.' Makes me feel antediluvian."

It was only since his daughter's arrival that the nearly twenty year age difference between him and his bride had begun to loom large. He'd reluctantly awakened to the fact that Mariana was Selina's contemporary. And if Mariana had called him 'sir' before that day, damned if he'd ever noticed it.

"I'm sorry." Lady Fawcett gave up the struggle to appear casual and put her hoop down on the work table.

There were many people who'd predicted that this May-December romance was predoomed to difficulty, but Mariana herself had not been of their number. She had fallen in love with Lord Fawcett on first sight. She considered him quite the handsomest man of her acquaintance. She adored his classic features, his clear gray eyes, and his fair, wavy hair, which he wore swept forward in a stylish Brutus cut that helped disguise his thinning temples. Except that she'd much preferred his maturity to the callowness of the younger men who'd dangled after her, age had been no factor in their relationship.

But far less obtuse than her husband, she was only too well aware of how they had both changed since coming back to England. This latest upset was indicative of an ever-widening rift.

"I believe you were going to tell me what I've done that is so dreadful—Aubrey." She had just managed to bite off the offending "sir" in time. "I had thought you'd be pleased, for the sake of Lady Selina and her friend, to have some other people in the household. I fear the young ladies must find us a trifle dull." She tried to keep any note of censure from her voice.

"Yes, I'm sure you acted for the best, m'dear." His

3

lordship's eyes softened as they rested on the petite young girl. He still could not believe his luck in winning such a beauty. But Mariana was beginning to look rather drawn, he noticed. Her normally large blue eyes now appeared enormous. The alabaster skin he so admired was surely rather too pale. He frowned at the ribboned cap she was wearing in an attempt to look mature. It all but hid the blond ringlets that he loved. Confound it, they should have stayed in Venice another month. It was too soon to plunge a girl of her age into all this domestic hubbub.

"I just wish you had consulted me before you asked anyone to stay, that's all."

She didn't feel that she could tell him just what it was like being sent to Coventry while he was called away on business for two days. Or how she'd longed for some company who did not despise her. Instead she said defensively, "I didn't dream that you'd object to having our neighbor come stay with us. I had understood that Lady Harriet Fane was a close family friend. Is it my brother then that you'd prefer not to see, sir?" She could have sunk with mortification when her voice began to quiver.

"No, no, of course not. Don't be absurd." Lord Fawcett spoke a bit too heartily. The truth was, he did find Lieutenant Soame Townshend something of a here-and-therein and wasn't eager to expose Selina and her friend to his rather raffish brand of charm. "You must know perfectly well, m'dear, that any member of your family is always welcome here."

"Then it must be Colonel Melford whom you object to." Her eyes grew wide. "But when Soame asked to bring the colonel along, I thought that you'd be pleased. He told me that you two are old acquaintances, belong to the same clubs, hunted together, all that sort of thing. And I thought that the young ladies might enjoy having another unattached gentleman around. I never dreamed you'd find him objectionable."

"Oh, *I* don't find him objectionable. Under other circumstances there's nothing I'd like better than to entertain Rawdon Melford. Why the man's a nonesuch. A bruising rider—well bound to be that, cavalry, of course, like your brother. He's an expert whip, strips with the Fancy. And, lord, you should see the cove play cricket!" But then his lordship's small flame of enthusiasm flickered and went out. "No, it ain't me that'll find Sir Rawdon objectionable. Harriet Fane will be the one for that."

"Lady Harriet? You mean she knows him?"

"Knows him! Good lord, child, they were betrothed. Had an announcement in the *Gazette*. The whole thing. It had all been arranged, don't you see, since they were both in the infantry. Their estates marched together. Their fathers were fast friends. Everybody thought it a match made in heaven. Though why they'd think a thing like that is beyond me. From the word go the two were like that battling couple in *The Taming of the Shrew*. And when I said just now that Colonel Rawdon Melford's a nonesuch, well you can include his successes in the petticoat line. The blowup came when Lady Harriet caught him making love to another woman at their engagement party."

"You can't mean it," Lady Fawcett gasped. "How disgusting."

"Well no, actually, I don't mean *that*," her husband qualified. "They weren't having a roll on the floor of the conservatory, if that's what you're think-

5

ing. But he was kissing this female out in the garden when Harriet happened along and gave 'em a quick shove into the ornamental lake before they ever knew what hit them." Lord Fawcett chuckled wickedly at the recollection. "Then the next day she cried off. Which turned out to be a pity, actually," he added reflectively. "For that rackety father of hers speculated away everything they had. Harriet was practically a pauper when she'd settled up his debts after he'd died. And Rawdon's a nabob. Pity she couldn't have just blinked at all his womanizing. But that wouldn't have been in Harriet's nature. She's always been too high in the instep for her own good. Still, I have to give her credit. She's managing. Life in that pokey little cottage of hers is a terrible comedown from the Manor House, but she'd never let you know it. Too much pride by half. And she won't thank us, I'll tell you that right now, for throwing Rawdon Melford in her teeth."

"Oh dear." Mariana was looking even more stricken. "How long ago did all this happen?"

"Hmmm. It's hard to say." Fawcett frowned in concentration. "As I recall, Harriet was just out, still in her teens. And she's getting pretty long in the tooth now, though I must say she don't look it. but she can't be all that far from thirty."

"Well then, perhaps time will have healed the wounds."

"Humph! And perhaps pigs will fly!" her husband snorted. "No, it ain't in the nature of those two firebrands to forget a thing like that. Or in anybody else's nature, when it comes to that. I tell you, the gossip mongers had a circus. I always wondered if Rawdon didn't join the army just to escape the cackle. Anyhow," he returned to the central issue,

6

"throwing those two together here at Fairoaks is unthinkable. Best write your brother straight away and put 'em off."

"I'm afraid it's a bit too late for that," his bride replied miserably. "They're due here tomorrow."

"Oh dear God," he groaned. "Well, if that don't bring the roof down around our ears, nothing will."

Mariana, drowning, reached out to clutch a straw. "Of course, Soame was a little vague about the whole thing, actually. He wrote that he'd run into Colonel Melford at White's and that the Colonel mentioned having business here in Berkshire. So Soame told him he was going there himself and he was certain that his brother-in-law would be happy to put his friend up as well. But in point of fact, Soame didn't actually say that Colonel Melford had accepted the invitation."

"Oh?" Her spouse brightened. "Well, now I come to think on it, I can't imagine Rawdon Melford wanting to rusticate with a house full of dull dogs like us."

"Then perhaps he won't come after all."

Lady Fawcett's spoken words were quickly transformed into a silent prayer.

# Chapter
## Two

FAIROAKS HALL WAS asleep. At least it should have been. But seconds before, Catley the butler had shrugged, cursing, back into his coat to answer the front door bell. And the Fawcett's houseguest, being unable to settle for the night in an unfamiliar bed, was emerging from the library with an armful of soporific books at the very moment he did so. Colonel Sir Rawdon Melford stepped inside the hall and shook the rain drops from his beaver. Lady Harriet Fane dropped her stack of books.

The colonel turned her way and thoughtfully studied the tall, slender, nightgowned figure. The white ruffled nightcap that she wore, by contrast, made her eyes appear all the darker, and the soft candlelight failed to mute the reddish gold of the curls that escaped from underneath it. The colonel grinned as he stared pointedly at the volumes scattered round her slippered feet. "Well now, that's progress, Harry. A few years ago, you'd have chucked 'em at me."

"What the devil are you doing here?"

His eyebrows rose. "Is that any sort of language for a lady? What would your dear old governess say?"

"Never mind my dear old governess. Just why are you here, Major Melford?"

"*Colonel* Melford, actually. But I mustn't cavil. At least you've followed my career up to a point."

As Catley tactfully withdrew into the background, Lady Harriet gave the *colonel* a speaking look and tried to get a grip on her sensibilities.

The shock of seeing her ex-fiancé after so many years wasn't eased by the fact that time had only improved what had been a superior example of the male species to begin with. He'd filled out a bit, which, considering his towering height, was only to the good. The unfamiliar side whiskers and military mustache that complemented the mop of dark hair, now curling out of control from the dampness, gave him a mature, distinguished look, she conceded. Memory had not exaggerated the deep blue of his eyes. They always, she recalled, appeared to see too much. Right now they were laughing at her dishabille. The haughty tone she adopted was meant to compensate for her sartorial disadvantage.

"Congratulations on your promotion, sir. But you have not answered my question. What the devil are you doing here?"

"Visiting. I'm an invited guest. What are *you* doing here? Oh my God!" He broke off in consternation. "I heard that Fawcett married again. Don't tell me you're the bride."

"Of course not. But don't tell me you don't even know who your hostess is. That's rackety even for you, Rawdon."

He slapped his forehead. "Of course. It all comes back to me now. Can't think how I came to forget. Well, yes I can, actually. It was the shock of seeing you suddenly materialize. And dressed like that.

You can't begin to imagine how often I've pictured you in nightclothes, Harry. Though to tell the truth they were a great deal more diaphanous than that convent issue you're—"

"Rawdon! Colonel Melford, I mean to say!" Her tone was dangerous.

"Rawdon's fine. Seems a bit silly for us to stand on points, Harry."

"And don't call me Harry, Colonel Melford. And do, pray, try and explain why you're here. And at this ungodly hour."

"I'm here because Soame Townshend asked me. And, of course, now that I come to think on it, he was ladling out the hospitality because his sister's the one who married Fawcett. That clears me up. What are you doing here, Harry?"

"I'm a houseguest. I have a cottage nearby and Lord and Lady Fawcett asked me to come help them entertain his daughter and her friend. So you can't stay here."

The colonel looked pointedly around him at the enormous hall. The expanse of checkerboard marble gave a clue to the vast proportions of the house. "Short of bedchambers are they?" he inquired.

"Don't be absurd. You know perfectly well why you can't stay here."

"I know nothing of the kind. And, by the by, do we have to go on standing here? Couldn't we discuss it over a glass of port in the library there?"

Catley, who'd been dozing on his feet in the background, snapped to attention, then melted softly away.

"We could not," Lady Harriet replied with indignant emphasis. "Because you're leaving. There's a very good public house in the village with a few rooms for travelers. The Magpie, it's called. You'll be well taken care of."

"I know. I just came from there. It's why I'm late. But I've no intention of putting up at the Magpie. Weren't you listening? I'm invited to stay here."

"But I'm staying here," she said between clenched teeth. "And you must see that both of us can't possibly—"

"What I see is that you're about to indulge in another one of your harangues, and I'd like to get comfortable to hear it." Colonel Melford stepped over the pile of books to take Lady Harriet firmly by the arm and turn her toward the library. She was about to protest when the butler reappeared with a crystal decanter, two glasses, and some biscuits upon a silver tray. Rather than create a scene, she capitulated.

But once they were settled in the book-lined room in opposing wing backs before the empty Adam fireplace and he'd poured out the port, which she pointedly ignored, she resumed her diatribe. "Even you must see that we both can't stay here, Colonel Melford."

"Why ever not? Surely by now you've outgrown your odious habit of pushing people into pools. If not, I promise to be on my guard."

"Don't be so thick. You know perfectly well that this situation is intolerable."

"I know nothing of the kind. Except for the brief but stormy period of our betrothal, I would have said that we were the best of friends."

"Then you would have had maggots in your head. We were never friends."

"Now, dammit, I take exception to that. Oh, I grant you, we were always at daggers drawn. Or at least

11

you were. It's that fiery ginger hair that does it. Irish ancestry most likely, I'd say. Now, as I recall, I was always the soul of amiability. But you would insist upon dogging my steps when you'd no business to and on trying to outride and outshoot me, which of course you could never do."

"Oh I don't know about that. If my horse had not gone lame during that point-to-point when I was twelve—"

"Which you never could do," he repeated firmly. "And that fact always put your temper in a blaze. But setting aside your tantrums, I'd say that we've been friends since we both could toddle. By the by," he broke off, "may I say that you're looking splendid, Harry? Haven't changed a bit in all these years. At least not so as you could notice under that god-awful nightdress you're wearing."

"Don't try and foist your Spanish coin off on me, Rawdon Melford. Of course I've changed. And it's a long time since I've toddled. I'm twenty-seven."

"Twenty-seven! Tsk, tsk," he jeered. "Well, I can help you back up the stairs and I'm twenty-nine."

"You're thirty."

"Twenty-nine, and you'll soon be twenty-eight."

Harriet shook her head to clear it. It was impossible that she was actually sitting here in her nightclothes with Sir Rawdon Melford arguing about their ages. She might have, in her weaker moments, occasionally wondered just what it would be like to see him again, but never in her wildest—

"All right," she interrupted her jumbled thoughts, "you're twenty-nine. But our respective ages have nothing at all to say in the matter. The only point here is that we can't both stay under the same roof and you'll have to go."

"I beg respectfully to differ. Our ages are germane to the issue, I'd say. Its' been—what?—eight years now?—since you made a complete cake of yourself at our engagement party."

Her dark eyes shot sparks. *"I* make a cake of *myself?"*

"That's what I said."

"Why you philandering nodcock! How you could have the gall to sit there and say—? But never mind." She reined in her temper. "No need to go into all that again. The point is, no one's likely to have forgotten our past association, and your remaining here can only prove awkward and embarrassing for everyone. So go!"

"I can't go," he replied patiently. "Even if I had the inclination to approach my host and hostess and say, 'Look here, I'm sorry, but I refuse to reside under the same roof with my hoydenish ex-fiancée—' "

"Take care!" she snarled.

"Just what kind of a sap skull would they take me for? And may I add that although our little contretemps may be uppermost in your mind, you flatter yourself if you think anybody else remembers or gives a damn."

"And you delude yourself if you believe any scandal is ever forgotten. But never mind that, for you don't have to say anything at all to your host and hostess. They retired ages ago. Simply turn around, go back to the Magpie, and write a note tomorrow crying off. You've been called back to London on urgent business. Nothing could be simpler."

"Except for one thing. I've been trying to tell you. I can't go to the Magpie."

"I know it's late, but beat on the door till they open up, for heaven's sake."

"Oh, it ain't the hour. It's Shaftoe's true love that's the problem there. You do remember Shaftoe, our head groom's son?"

"Of course I remember Shaftoe. He was your boon companion when we were children. But as usual you're making my head spin. What does Jem Shaftoe have to say in the matter?"

"A lot, actually. He's the reason for my being here. He's fallen head over heels in love with Old Flack's daughter. Flack owns the Magpie, you see."

"I know that. I happen to live in Mitford, remember?"

"Well, Shaftoe's pining over Rosina Flack. Can't say as I blame him. She's a fetching little thing." He looked positively lascivious for a moment, and her eyes narrowed. "But the thing is, you see, Old Flack's taken a decidedly dim view of his only child walking out with a valet."

"Shaftoe's your valet? I'll not believe it! Your groom, perhaps, but *valet*? Never!"

"Why ever not? He's a regular Brummel when it comes to clothes. Oh I grant you, he ain't the usual type. But after the war—we went through the whole thing together, you see—we were left at loose ends, so to speak, not eager to settle down."

"Humph," she sniffed. "Were you ever?"

"Why yes, as a matter of fact. Eight years ago . . . . But as I was saying, Shaftoe and I traveled around quite a bit, and we happened to stop at the Magpie. The poor devil was done in at first sight. Now the thing is, he wants to be in the same neighborhood with Miss Flack without making it obvious he's come here on her account. Besides her father's attitude, you see, he's up against the fact that the girl's a shocking flirt. The more males the merrier, that's

14

her attitude. He's trying to be crafty, don't you see, and not let her know she could add his scalp to the others dangling from her belt.

"So when Soame Townshend happened to mention he was coming here, it seemed the very thing. I wheedled an invitation, and here we are, strategically placed to pursue the landlord's daughter. Not 'we' but Shaftoe, I mean, of course," he amended as her eyebrows rose. "So that's why I can't leave here, even if I were so inclined, which I ain't, I assure you. For it would be a rotten turn to serve on Shaftoe. He saved my life in the Peninsula, don't you know. So sorry, old girl, you'll just have to make the best of a sticky matter."

Lady Harriet Fane rose to her feet. Rawdon looked her up and down appreciatively, his long legs stretched toward the fireplace fender as if in search of an absent blaze. "You've made a devilish pretty woman, Harry. Unless, of course," he grinned, "I'm blinded by the port."

"Please do not keep calling me Harry. No, never mind that. You won't be calling me anything. For if you refuse to leave, well, then I shall have to return home myself tomorrow."

He shrugged. "Well, suit yourself, of course. But it seems a damned silly thing to do if you ask me."

"I didn't."

"Unless, of course," he mused, "you're afraid of falling in love with me all over again."

"Our marriage was *arranged,* if you recall," she said witheringly. "I was never in love with you."

"Oh no? Then why the devil did you push me in the drink?"

"Someone had to do it," she shot back.

"Now I must bid you good night, sir. No, not good

night," she said over her shoulder as she swept regally from the room. "What I meant to say, actually, was good-bye."

The door closed behind her. The colonel poured himself another glass of port and sipped its contents thoughtfully, while on the other side of the thick oak portal Catley sat down upon a hall settee and nodded.

# Chapter
# Three

Lady harriet had intended to make her excuses bright and early the next morning and then leave the Hall. But her interview with Rawdon Melford had caused her to toss and turn for most of the night and, finally, to oversleep. It was well after ten when she entered the breakfast parlor. She noted with relief that the colonel was not there. Neither was her hostess, which was not surprising. Lady Fawcett would have duties to attend to.

While she helped herself to sweetbreads and toast at the sideboard, Harriet could not avoid noting the strained atmosphere. Her host was buried in the newspaper, and, except for a perfunctory greeting when she'd entered, seemed intent upon shutting out his surroundings. His daughter and friend were as far removed from him as the small table would allow. Lady Harriet chose a spot that bridged the distance. After one polite attempt at conversation had died aborning, she was glad enough to abandon the notion of sociability. While appearing to focus all her attention on her plate, she surreptitiously studied the young ladies.

It was fortunate, she thought, that Lady Selina

had inherited her looks from her father. Fair, with large gray eyes and regular features, she came close to beauty, a quality that her mother had lacked. It was a pity, though, that Selina had not inherited that lady's amiability. A sullen expression when she stole glances at her father threatened to undo all nature's handiwork.

Her friend, Miss Susan Tunstall, had seemed a lively sort on first acquaintance. Now the tension between father and daughter was having a dampening effect upon her vivacity, if not her appetite. Miss Tunstall was devouring boiled eggs and ham with considerable relish. She, too, was a pretty girl, slightly plump, with dark hair and eyes, a foil for Selina.

While Harriet watched beneath lowered lids, Lady Selina whispered something in her companion's ear. Miss Tunstall cut her eyes toward his lordship and stifled a giggle. Harriet wondered with a pang if she'd ever been that young and silly. Eager to escape what was obviously a family falling out, she speeded up her breakfast.

She was rapidly disposing of the final sweetbread while marveling at the appetite of Miss Tunstall who was making another trip to the sideboard, when Rawdon Melford came striding into the room. His entrance forced Lord Fawcett to put down his paper and rise to his feet. "Oh there you are, Colonel. Catley told me you arrived last night."

A sudden crash came from the sideboard. All eyes turned to Miss Tunstall who had dropped her plate. Her gaze was riveted upon Colonel Melford. Her expression could have illustrated a lurid, horrid mystery.

"Susan!" the colonel exclaimed, looking understandably a bit unsettled. "I'd no notion I'd see you here."

Miss Tunstall's face was a study in transformation. It evolved from shocked to stormy in record time. Angry tears were observed gathering in her eyes. "Fustian!" she all but shouted at the colonel. "I'm not a fool, you know. Mama has sent you to spy on me. Well, I'll have you understand that I'm no longer a child, Sir Rawdon." And she went running from the room as the tears spilled over. Lady Selina shot an accusing look at her father, then jumped up and followed.

"Good God! What was that all about?" Lord Fawcett demanded. A footman hurried to clean up the mess.

"Dashed if I know. Must be something in the air here. Every female who claps eyes on me immediately drops whatever's in her hands."

Lady Harriet laughed and received a set-down look from her former fiancé. Sir Rawdon collapsed in a chair across the table from her and asked for coffee.

"I may take it, then, that you and the young lady are well acquainted?" she prodded.

"Not all that well. But I am her guardian."

"*You!* A young lady's guardian?" Lady Harriet choked suddenly. "Isn't that a bit like appointing the fox to guard the henhouse?"

Even Lord Fawcett chuckled. "I must say that's news to me," he said. "I didn't know that you and Miss Tunstall were acquainted, let alone related."

"Oh, I remember now," Lady Harriet offered. "Those Yorkshire relations you used to visit when we were children, weren't they Tunstalls?"

"That's right." Colonel Melford had recovered

enough to visit the sideboard. "Geoffrey—that's Susan's father—was my first cousin," he explained over his shoulder as he filled his plate. "When he took ill, he named me the girl's guardian. Her mama's a good enough sort, but a bit flighty. She's remarried now, though, and Susan's stepfather is a sound, steady chap and quite good with the children. Treats Susan no differently from his own. So what with that and my having been rather occupied with Napoleon these last few years, I really haven't done much in the way of guardianship. But I shouldn't have thought that would have put the girl into such a taking. Dammit, I've remembered all her birthdays." He sounded rather hurt.

"She's probably just oblivious to your charms. There just possibly could be females like that, you know." Harriet put down her napkin and rose to her feet. "Now if you gentlemen will excuse me."

They watched her go in silence. Then, "Women!" the colonel muttered.

"Right," his host agreed. "Complete waste of time to try and figure why they do what they do. Now take that little scene with your ward. She probably doesn't even know herself what brought it on. Maybe it's just the age. If my own daughter's anything to go by, seventeen's impossible. Selina's got the body of a woman and the temperament of a child." He seemed ready to expand upon this theme but took a thoughtful sip of tea before confiding, "I don't mind saying, Rawdon, for you're bound to notice it, that since I remarried, she's made my life hell. And damned if I know why. It ain't as if her mother's not yet cold in her grave or anything like that. I'd been a widower for three long years, dammit, when I met Mariana.

And a sweeter, more amiable girl you'll not find anywhere."

"Oh, you're to be congratulated on the match," the colonel replied warmly. "Lady Fawcett stopped by my chamber earlier to welcome me, and she's a nonpareil, without question." He dampened down his enthusiasm, however, as his host gave him a suspicious look. It occurred to Rawdon, not for the first time, that his reputation with the ladies had become quite overblown. Then, too, Lord Fawcett was older than his bride. And in the colonel's experience, that tended to make husbands a bit touchy. "I should have thought," he went on to say, "that Lady Fawcett and your daughter would have got on like a house afire." He could have kicked himself immediately for the gaffe.

"Since they're of an age, you mean?" his host replied testily.

"No, no. By George, are they? I should not have thought—that is to say, her ladyship seems much more mature, don't you know."

"Well, actually, she's twenty. Almost."

"Oh, well then. There you are. There's a big gulf between twenty and seventeen. As you were just saying, at seventeen they may look like women, but they're children at heart.

"I expect the problem is, your daughter's a bit jealous. She's probably thought of you as her sole property. Does she have a sweetheart?"

"No. At least," his lordship qualified, "none that I know of."

"That's it, then. As soon as she fixes her interest on someone else, I'll bet a monkey all her jealousy of your bride will evaporate like morning dew."

"Do you think so?"

"I'm sure of it."

Lord Fawcett was visibly brightening. "By Jove, you could just be right. I must own it would be a relief to have the girl settled in her own household. Things just haven't been the same with Mariana and me since we came back." He sighed and stirred his tea reflectively. "By the by, where the deuce is Soame? I thought you and he were coming down together."

"He got delayed. Business, so he said. Told me to come on ahead. Hope you don't mind, Fawcett."

"No, no, of course not. Just seems a rather rackety way for him to act. But then—" He left the thought unfinished.

"Oh Soame's a bit on the harum-scarum side, I'll grant you, but he's a capital fellow. Would give his right arm for you in a pinch. Were you perhaps thinking . . . ?"

"Of Soame Townshend and Selina? Good God, no. That would never do."

"Oh I see." Actually he didn't, but he tactfully dropped the subject. The two men focused their attention for a bit upon their plates.

"By the by, Rawdon," his lordship rather awkwardly broke the silence as he buttered a piece of toast, "I do owe you an apology."

"You do? Whatever for?"

"Well, I know it can't be exactly comfortable being thrown together with Lady Harriet this way. After all that business in the past. The thing is, you see, my Mariana didn't know about all the scan—that is to say, she doesn't know our local history. She meant well, of course. But her ignorance has put the two of you in a deuced awkward situation."

22

"Not a bit of it," the other protested stoutly. "That's all water under the bridge now. I don't doubt that Harriet's forgiven and forgotten the whole business years ago."

"Hmmm," was his lordship's only comment.

But his inner reflection was that if Colonel Sir Rawdon Melford, baronet, really believed the nonsense he was spouting, not only was his reputation as a lady's man quite undeserved, he was something of a fool as well.

# Chapter
## Four

LADY SELINA RUSHED into the bedchamber after her friend. She found her there sobbing, facedown, upon the four-poster bed.

"Susan, whatever's the matter?" Alarmed, she climbed up beside the distressed young lady and patted her ineffectually on the shoulder. "I've never seen you like this. Who is that man?"

"My gu-guardian," came the muffled answer.

"Oh good heavens!"

There was a long period of near silence while Selina frowned, and Susan sniffled. "What on earth can he be doing here?" the former mused.

"Do you even have to ask?" Susan rolled over and sat up, blotting her eyes with the bed curtains. "Isn't it obvious? Mama sent him."

"I can't believe it. I don't think your mother suspects a thing."

Susan gave her friend a withering look. "Next you'll be saying that his being here is simply a co-incidence."

"I won't say anything of the kind, for I've never even heard of the fellow."

"You mean he's never been here before?"

"Not to my knowledge, and I'm not likely to forget a thing like that. He's certainly handsome, isn't he? Why did you never tell me that you have a guardian who's an absolute Adonis?"

"Selina!"

"Oh very well then. But I still insist that your mama never suspected a thing. Good God!" She broke off sharply. "Of course! That's it! Mariana!"

"Whatever do you mean?"

"Why, it's obvious. Your mother didn't set him on us, for she hasn't a clue. And he's no friend of *our* family to show up like this out of the blue. So there's only one answer." Her eyes narrowed angrily. "It has to be Mariana. She's somehow found out and sent for him." She slid off the bed.

"Where are you going?"

"To have a word with my stepmama." Her lip curled over the word. "For if your guardian doesn't turn out to be her bosom bow, well then, I'm a Frenchie."

Lady Harriet Fane was in a quandary. She knew perfectly well what she should do—run for cover. That was the prudent way to deal with the conflicting emotions that Rawdon Melford had once more roused.

She would never have dreamed she could still feel so much anger after all these years. She would have sworn she was over and done with that sort of thing long ago. Anger was not the worst of it, however. She could cope with anger. What she couldn't cope with was the fact that she still considered him the most attractive man she had ever met.

The most attractive *scoundrel,* she amended. For a leopard could not have changed its spots in a mere eight years. She was sure of that much. Oh yes, she was definitely going to seek the sanctuary of her own cottage. Still—there was the matter of her strained budget. A fortnight here at the Hall would certainly help. Blast Rawdon, anyhow! Why did he have to show up just when she'd gotten her life more or less on an even keel?

As she strode toward her bedchamber, Harriet was so deep in thought that she passed the servant in the hall without consciously seeing him. But then the image registered. She turned with her hand closed upon the doorknob. "Shaftoe, is that you?"

"Yes, m'lady." The valet, his arms piled high with the colonel's freshly laundered linen, stopped in his tracks. "Didn't think you remembered me."

"How could I possibly forget you?" Harriet replied warmly as she walked toward him. "I was—preoccupied."

"I expect so, miss." There was a knowing look in the valet's eyes.

She appraised him now carefully, thinking what a nice-looking man he'd become with his chiseled features, his light brown hair, and his intelligent gray eyes. He was a bit shorter than she was, forced to look up and meet her gaze. He was slightly built and wiry, but the well-cut dark clothes he wore did not disguise a muscular physique. "You've changed very little, Shaftoe," she summed up.

"Especially in stature." His laugh was not echoed in his eyes.

He's sensitive about his height, she realized. Comes from spending so much time waiting on a giant.

The two reminisced a bit under the curious eyes of an upstairs maid who was popping in and out of bedchamber doors as she tidied. After Lady Harriet had inquired after Shaftoe's father and several other of the Melford servants whom she had known, she lowered her voice to ask, "Tell me, Jem, what does Rawdon's ward have against him?"

The valet's eyes grew wide. "Why nothing that I know of, your ladyship. I just heard this morning in servants' hall that Miss Tunstall's a guest here. I would have supposed she'd be very glad to see the colonel. It's been quite a while since we've visited her family, of course, but their relationship was always most cordial. In fact, I'd go so far as to say there was a bit of hero worship on her part."

"Well, then it must have been the uniform," Lady Harriet said dryly. "For from her reaction this morning, he could have been an ogre—of the most unpleasant sort." She went on then to describe the scene she'd witnessed.

"Now that is odd," the valet mused. "You're certain, m'lady, that she used the phrase 'spy on me'?"

"Positive."

"Hmmm. Sounds as if Miss Susan's up to something."

"I'd certainly say so."

"Well I'll keep my eyes and ears both open, your ladyship."

"Do that, Shaftoe. It's Colonel Melford's responsibility, of course, but, well—" she shrugged.

"Aren't you rather hard on him, miss?" The gray eyes held a touch of censure.

"Not a bit of it. But I do admire your loyalty, Shaftoe. And it's nice to see you again. Give my best to your father when you see him." With a dismissive smile, she turned and entered her room.

Harriet had started for the bellpull to summon a

maid to pack her things, when she hesitated. Best to make her excuses to her hostess first.

She had to knock twice on Lady Fawcett's door before a muffled voice bade her to come in. And even though her ladyship was on her feet with a smile fixed in place when Harriet stepped inside, it was immediately obvious, and not just from the rumpled counterpane, that she'd been sprawled upon the bed, in tears.

"Oh, dear," Harriet blurted, "I've chosen a bad time, haven't I?"

"Not a bit of it. I was just coming to see you. Do have a seat." Mariana indicated a chair pulled up in front of a casement window. She herself sat down on the window seat. "I realize that I owe you an apology, you see, and wish to make it."

"An apology? But that's absurd."

"You're very kind, and I do appreciate it. But there's no need to pretend that I haven't made the most dreadful faux pas in asking Colonel Melford here. But the thing I'm most anxious to convince you of, Lady Harriet, is that I acted out of ignorance, not maliciousness."

"My heavens, Mariana—may I call you Mariana? And please do address me as Harriet—you don't have to convince me of that. I'm certain you're incapable of maliciousness."

"That doesn't seem to be the generally held opinion." Mariana's brave attempt at a smile was a dismal failure. "But the simple truth is, it was my brother Soame's idea to invite the colonel. Though I will admit it sounded like a splendid idea to me. As you may know, the colonel and Aubrey are acquainted and have a great deal in common, although Aubrey is a bit older, of course. What I did not know," she said emphatically, "was his connection with you and Miss Tunstall."

"Well, never mind his connection with me." Harriet eased her chair a bit closer. "I must own I was amazed at Miss Tunstall's rather violent reaction. Do you know the cause of it?"

The other shook her head. "All I know is what Selina says, that Miss Tunstall deeply resents his being here and—" again there was a threat of tears—"they seem to think I've somehow invited him to be spiteful. But I assure you, I had no idea that the colonel was such a wrong 'un. When I met him this morning, he seemed quite charming."

"Well, he isn't. That is to say," Harriet interpreted, "he isn't a wrong 'un. At least not in the way you mean. Oh dear," she smiled ruefully. "If I'm making a terrible muddle of this, it's because I'm totally unused to defending Rawdon Melford and it's an uncomfortable role for me. But the point is, that business between him and me has nothing to say in this other matter. In fact, Miss Tunstall's reaction came, I understand, as a total, unexpected shock to the colonel. His contacts with his ward have been of a rather erratic nature, so I've been told, but have always been quite cordial." She went on then to share a little of the conversation she'd had with the valet. "So it does appear that in this instance the colonel is quite innocent. And it leads me to suspect that there's something a bit rotten in Denmark. Have you any notion of what Miss Tunstall might be up to?"

"None in the least. But then I wouldn't. I'm hardly in the young ladies' confidence."

"In fact," Harriet said shrewdly, "Selina has been making your life miserable, hasn't she?"

The other made no attempt to deny it. "I've tried

very hard to be friends. But she resents me deeply. No, not to put too fine a point on it, she loathes me. She thinks her father was a fool to marry me. And frankly," her voice quivered, "I'm becoming of the same opinion."

"Nonsense. You're the best thing that ever happened to Aubrey. Why, I've never seen him so happy. He looked ten years younger when you first came home." Oh dear. She did wish she'd chosen her words more carefully.

Mariana picked up on them. "That still would make him ten years older than I am," she sighed. "Besides, you're speaking of the way he looked before we settled in."

"You mean before Selina came back home, don't you?"

"Well, yes, in part. But there's more to it than that. It's everything. I've had no experience in running a house the size of Fairoaks, don't you see, with all these servants. And, frankly, I find it overpowering. Everything I try to do seems to be wrong—upsets some custom of the first Lady Fawcett. Now this business of Colonel Melford is simply the last straw. I know that Aubrey regrets the day he went down on one knee to me."

"Fustian."

"No, it's true." The tears were taking over. "He's changed entirely since we've come home. Italy was so marvelous."

"Well I couldn't say from firsthand experience, of course, but I expect every marriage experiences some letdown after the honeymoon. Would have to, I'd think."

"It's not just that. He treats me like a child now. Which he did not do before, I assure you. He's come to realize that I'm not the wife he should have chosen to be mistress here."

"My heavens, Mariana, you can't expect to build Rome in a day. Believe me, most brides would be daunted by this place."

"You wouldn't be. I understand that your former home was even grander."

"That was all some time ago. Besides which, it has nothing to say in the matter."

"It has in a way. Selina says that her father should have married you."

"Oh did she indeed!" Harriet snapped. "Well, I assure you such a thought never entered Aubrey's head. Or mine. And let me assure you of one thing more, Mariana. Selina would have resented anybody who married her father. Oh, the age difference gives her a nice bone of contention to gnaw on, I'll grant you, but Aubrey could have married someone twenty years his senior, and she'd still be jealous."

"Fustian. But I thank you," the other smiled.

"All right then, I'm doing it a bit too brown, I'll admit. You're young and pretty, and that makes her jealousy a lot worse. But that's her problem and not your fault. The truth is—though I shouldn't speak ill of the dead—her mother spoiled her terribly. Maria couldn't have any more children, as you may know, and she had enough maternal instinct to smother a dozen. But except for that," she said in a rallying tone, "Selina's not impossible. She really does have some good points, though I must say they've been well hidden of late. But give her time. She'll come around."

"Oh you are a good friend!" Mariana impulsively clasped the other's hand and squeezed it gratefully. "You've made me feel much better, you know. Except that now I'm even more sorry that I've put you in such an awkward position by inviting Colonel Melford here. And I want you to know I quite understand your leaving. That is what you came in here to tell me, isn't it?"

"Why no, not a bit of it," Harriet lied. "I just dropped by to offer you my assistance in organizing your ball. I think it's a splendid idea to celebrate Aubrey's birthday," she prevaricated even further. For in truth, she doubted that Fawcett would feel exactly festive over turning forty. "But I'm wondering if it's really wise to surprise him. Gentlemen, in my observation, don't often take to surprises very well."

"Oh but that was Selina's suggestion. In fact, the notion of giving a ball was hers as well." The tears welled up once more in Lady Fawcett's eyes. "I should have known, of course, that she was merely making mischief."

Lady Harriet, with some difficulty, restrained herself from marching straight into Selina's bedchamber and boxing that young lady's ears.

# Chapter
# Five

IT WAS MIDAFTERNOON when Jem Shaftoe sauntered down the street toward the Magpie Inn. He eyed the edifice with a decided lack of appreciation. It was a whitewashed building set back from the road a bit. Its swinging sign had been newly painted. Shaftoe's opinion was that the feathered fowl looked more like a duck than the bird intended. And the bow window that adorned one side of the building should have been made larger, he concluded. But even as he criticized he was well aware of the source of his jaundiced attitude. This admittedly thriving establishment would one day be the property of Miss Flack.

That should have been a cause for celebration. God knows, he wished Rosina well. But, in point of fact, her prospects were a thorn in Shaftoe's side. Not only did they give Miss Flack an inflated estimate of her own worth, which considering nature's favors would have been bad enough, they made her formidable father label every male who looked her way (with the exception of Farmer Holton) a fortune hunter.

Shaftoe ran his eyes over the inn yard. There were only two carts waiting there. Rosina should have a bit of time on her hands. He opened the door and went inside.

It took a moment for his eyes to adjust from bright exterior sunshine to interior gloom. They were pulled first, by lover's instinct, to the alcove beyond the bar where one of the booths was occupied. Though her back was toward him, he instantly recognized the dark ringlets of Miss Flack. (In this one respect, nature had let her down. The coiffure was the result of an uncomfortable night spent in curl papers.) The gentleman with her, who was eliciting frequent giggles by some tale he told, was unknown to him, however. Shaftoe's eyes narrowed. He went to join the two cart owners at the bar.

The landlord took his time polishing the glass he was drying while he eyed the newcomer askance. Missing was the cordiality he was famed for. "Wot'll it be?" he asked eventually as the gleaming glass joined a row of dingy fellows behind the bar.

"A pint," was the equally laconic answer, and the landlord turned to draw it. His red waistcoat had been let out before, but from the way it strained at its newer seams, it was ripe for further expansion. A tribute to the inn's prosperity, Shaftoe concluded glumly.

He sipped the dark contents of his glass and concentrated upon not staring at the booth where the giggles had increased in frequency and volume, a sign that he'd been spotted. He used the time to scrutinize the young man next to him.

Two things made him almost sure of the cove's identity. One was that his sunburned face, calloused hands, and burly physique (not to mention a faint aroma of fertilizer) bespoke the farmer. The more telling clue was that his total attention was fixed

34

upon the booth. This, then, must be Joel Holton. And he must be lovesick indeed to have deserted his crops at this hour of the day.

The landlord had moved to stand in front of his other customer, an octogenarian who sucked toothlessly and loudly upon his mug. Their talk, which drifted up the bar, concerned cricket. But like the farmer's, Mr. Flack's attention was mainly elsewhere. His eyes traveled frequently toward the booth, and he frowned with displeasure. It wasn't long before he interrupted the old man's account of the prowess of the '98 eleven to bark, "Rosina! Joel's empty!"

While Joel Holton tried his best to look indifferent, out of the corners of his eyes Jem Shaftoe watched the booth. He would have wagered all he owned that it was on the tip of Miss Flack's tongue to tell her father to draw the beer himself. But under the landlord's beetled glower, even the saucy Rosina was not quite that brave. She tossed her curls, muttered something to her companion, then flounced behind the bar where she took the farmer's glass without a word and filled it—mostly with foam, Shaftoe noted. As she set the glass down with a thud, the farmer's none-too-intelligent face took on the aspect of an injured puppy. Despite the fact that it was his prosperous rival who was being discomforted, there was something about the incident that made Shaftoe long to apply the sole of his boot to his truelove's shapely rump.

His annoyance was fueled, not appeased, by the flirtatious smile she then flashed his way. He was well aware that the little doxy was bent on infuriating her father, while further tormenting the smitten farmer. Nor was she quite willing to let any other admirer wiggle off her hook. Shaftoe gave her a level look that conveyed he was well aware of all these things and had the satisfaction of seeing the smooth, olive complexion redden. "The same again," he said evenly.

Avoiding her father's eyes, Miss Flack left the bar to rejoin the gentleman. The ancient customer droned on, and the suitors sipped in silence for a bit. Then Shaftoe caught the farmer's eye and inquired softly, "Who's the gentrymort?"

Since his own mind was obviously fixed on the same gentleman, the farmer did not appear to find the question odd. "Major Mortram's his name," he muttered. "Though as to his business, I couldn't say."

"A stranger here, is he?"

"That's right. Drove his own rig in here three days ago. And 'e don't seem in any particular hurry to move on. Told Mr. Flack there," he nodded toward the landlord, "that he's just out of the army and wants to see some of the country before he settles down. But if you ask me, it ain't the scenery that's keeping him here."

"Hmmm. Did he say what his regiment was?" It could be simple prejudice, Shaftoe realized, that made him doubt the stranger's bona fides. Still, it was easy enough to stick "Major" in front of your name.

"I haven't talked to him." The tone implied that Mr. Holton could do without that pleasure.

"Regular Casanova, ain't he?" The valet covertly sized up the competition. Major Mortram had auburn hair, hazel eyes, and a Greek-god profile. Shaftoe had not the slightest doubt that the seated man was tall.

"I don't like it one bit, him sniffing around Rosina

that way," the farmer growled. "A gentleman like that. There's no mistaking the sort of thing he'd have in mind. But you can't tell the silly gudgeon anything. Thinks she's a prime catch, she does, and that even royalty's intentions would be honorable."

"Women!" Shaftoe muttered sympathetically, then took a long swig of beer.

The octogenarian got up and shuffled out the door, and the landlord came over to polish the bar in front of his other customers. "Have you two met?" he asked. "Mr. Holton here's a farmer. Owns a nice piece of land east of Mitford. Been in his family for generations, ain't that right, Joel? And Mr. Shaftoe here's stopping up at the Hall. He dresses a gentleman who's visiting his lordship. Makes sure his cravat's tied just so. Ain't that right, Mr. Shaftoe?"

"That's right," the other replied evenly, refusing to rise to the bait.

"Went all through the war with your gentleman, they tell me, seeing to it he got his tea served proper like."

Repressing an urge to pin the landlord's mouth shut with the medal he'd won for valor, Shaftoe merely nodded.

"And speaking of your gentleman, one of his lordship's stable lads was in here last night bragging that the colonel's a prime cricketer. Said he'd most likely be playing with Fawcett's eleven. That so, is it?"

"It's so about the colonel's ability. I haven't heard about the other."

"Well now, I don't expect you would have. Cricket wouldn't be exactly your cup of tea, now would it, Mr. Shaftoe?" Mr. Flack, who wasn't as conscious as Lady Harriet had been of the valet's muscular physique, gave the small man a contemptuous look.

"I enjoy the sport."

"Ha, that's a good one, that is, Joel. He *enjoys* the sport. While seeing to it his master don't get grass stains on his breeches, I wouldn't doubt." He guffawed at his own wit.

"Well, Mr. Shaftoe, I can tell you this much," the publican continued once he'd recovered, "Joel here is a champion bowler and the star of our village team, he is."

Mr. Holton tried unsuccessfully to look modest while he cut his eyes Rosina's way to see if she was listening.

"And I hope you don't mind me saying further that if your colonel does decide to play, he'll be no match for Joel here. Nor for any other of our Mitford lads when it comes to that."

Mr. Flack, who was something of a republican, went on to develop a favorite theme. "For it's been my experience, in spite of any remarks the Duke of Wellington might have made about the playing fields of Eton, that your gentry types may show well enough while they're playing one another, but they can't hold a candle to your good, honest, physically developed working man. [Here Shaftoe tried to imagine the old tub of lard at play and his mind boggled.] No, indeed, being a gentleman has its advantages, no doubt about it, but they don't show up on the cricket grounds. Rosina!" He interrupted his egalitarian lecture with a whoop. "Meg wants you in the kitchen."

"I didn't hear her call," his daughter answered.

"You heard *me*, though, didn't you?"

Miss Flack tossed her pretty head defiantly, but

obediently disappeared. Deprived of his companion, the gentleman stranger tossed off the contents of his glass, then ambled toward the bar. Damn, he was tall, Shaftoe noted.

"Did I hear you discussing cricket?" the gentleman inquired politely.

The major perched on a bar stool while Shaftoe sized up his sartorial splendor. To a less practiced eye, the bottle-green coat might have passed for Bond Street. But the valet was quick to recognize the telltale signs of inferior tailoring. He also found the major's shirt points a touch too high, his cravat a touch too intricate, and his adornments—fob, stick pin, rings and buttonhole—quite overdone. Too flashy by half was his conclusion.

"Yes, indeed, cricket was our subject," the landlord was saying. "We were discussing what the village's chances might be against the Hall when we play our annual match. The valet here says his gentleman is a nonesuch. Whilst I was pointing out that Mr. Holton here has few peers, if any, in the sport."

"Indeed?" The major gave the farmer an admiring look. "Well, now, I'd certainly like to be a spectator at that contest. For while I don't wish to appear immodest," he said, missing his stated intention by a mile, "I've had some small success in that game myself. In the army, that is, not at Lord's," he smiled.

As the major began an account of a match in which he seemed predestined to play the hero's part, Shaftoe emptied his glass and murmured his farewells, almost unnoticed.

When he emerged once more into the sunlight, he was not in the least surprised to spy Miss Flack in the courtyard, next to the stables. She was engaged in weeding a tub of geraniums that did not appear to require so much attention. He ambled over. "Waiting for me, then were you, love?"

The curls tossed from habit, and the dark eyes flashed. "You are a one to flatter yourself, aren't you, Mr. Shaftoe?"

"No, not really. I'm just more or less a student of human nature. So I guessed you'd want some audience reaction to the little show you put on back in there." He jerked a thumb at the Magpie.

"Well you've got some nerve, you have. Seems to me I was minding me own business. Which is a lot more, evidently, than some folk can say. I certainly wasn't trying to impress you, Jem Shaftoe."

"Oh not just me. I never thought it. You were trying to make your big clod of a farmer jealous, too."

Her face, which had been all indignation, switched to impishness. With one hand on her hip, she smiled provocatively. "And did it work in your case?"

Without answering, he took her roughly by the hand and whisked her inside the stable where he proceeded to kiss her long and ardently.

When he finally released her, gasping, he gazed into her flushed face and murmured, "It worked a fair treat, lass."

He was striding out the courtyard gate, whistling, before it even occurred to her that she should, by rights, have slapped him.

# Chapter
## Six

Rawdon melford was tempted to stop in at the Magpie as he rode one of his host's horses down the winding village street, but he resisted the temptation. He had little doubt that his valet had taken advantage of his absence to visit the delectable Rosina. It would be awkward for Shaftoe if he showed up.

So instead, he rode on past the inn, past the blacksmith's, past the village shop and reined in his bay before the cottage that had been his unacknowledged destination all along. He had no problem recognizing it from his host's description, except that he had not been sufficiently prepared for its lack of size. The colonel thought it a more fit habitat for dolls than human beings.

He was, however, appreciative of its spruce, well-kept appearance. Indeed, the fresh whitewash over brick looked almost defiant. As did the red geraniums in the casements. The riot of hollyhocks, roses, and honeysuckle in the small front garden forced him to breathe deeply of their fragrance. Oh there was no doubt about it, the place was simply awash

41

with charm. Sir Rawdon found it quite appalling. He dismounted, looped his reins over the gatepost, and walked slowly up the garden path.

When Lady Harriet Fane arrived home some twenty minutes later, she recognized Bonaparte, Lord Fawcett's stallion, and had a pretty fair idea of who the rider was. She guided her own borrowed mare around to the back of the garden and tethered her. Fighting to rein in her temper, she strode through the large glass folding doors that formed the entrance to an apartment variously called the summer room, the greenhouse, or the drawing room, depending on the residents' moods or the season. There she found Sir Rawdon comfortably ensconced in an easy chair with his riding boots resting on a leather ottoman. Miss Kate Russell, Harriet's elderly companion and former governess, was with him, separated by a small table heaped with tea things. Their chairs commanded a view of the flower-filled garden.

"Well, hullo there, Harry." Not bothering to rise, the colonel greeted her through a mouthful of cake. "Come in and have some ginger nuts. Nobody can match Miss Kate's ginger nuts. But then you'd know that, wouldn't you?"

"Do make yourself at home," the cottage owner said witheringly. "And for the thousandth time, don't call me Harry."

Miss Russell, a short, rotund lady in black bombazine, whose plumpness kept her amiable face almost wrinkle-free and left it up to the gray hair that peeked out from under her ruffled cap to betray her age, looked rather flustered. "Master Rawdon—oh for heaven's sake, would you just listen to me," she laughed nervously. "My, my, how time flies. Seems only yesterday he was a lad running in and out of the manor. But *Colonel Melford,* as I meant to say, and I were just talking over old times, Lady Harriet. Now if you'll excuse me, I'll fetch you a cup, and then there's the beans in the kitchen needing seen to."

Harriet took the vacated chair and silently watched the colonel wolf down ginger nuts while Miss Kate bustled back with cup and saucer and fresh tea.

"Can't see why my being here has to put you in such a pucker," Rawdon observed after they were alone and Harriet had had a restoring sip of her tea.

"Oh, can you not!"

"No, dammit, I can't. I was in the neighborhood and decided to drop in on Miss Kate. Always fond of the old girl, you could recall. And after all, *she* never broke our engagement."

"No, she wouldn't have." Harriet reached for the last ginger nut a fraction too late; he had scooped it off the plate. "Miss Kate's a romantic. She has a penchant for rogues."

"That's hard, Harry."

"Well, I find it a bit hard that you've sneaked over here to spy on me."

"Sneaked! I rode an iron-shod horse up the main street in broad daylight."

"Behind my back."

"My God, woman, I didn't know I had to have your permission to visit an old friend."

"Fustian! Oh I grant that you probably do have a soft spot for Miss Kate. But admit it, Rawdon, you were spying."

"Spying! Don't be so dashed dramatic. I will admit to some concern about your circumstances."

"Concern?" she mocked.

"Yes, dammit, concern. I seem to be rather more fond of you than you are of me. Understandable, I suppose. You never had much heart."

"And you had too much. Enough for every comely trollop in the country. But let's not start all that again. And to be quite fair, I don't suppose I should blame you if you've come to gloat."

"Gloat!" His face, incredulous at first, rapidly suffused with anger. "Just why the devil would I wish to gloat?"

"Human nature, certainly. I daresay it stung your pride a bit to be publicly rejected."

His steady gaze impaled her. "Oh my pride survived intact, Harry. As I recall, my satin knee smalls were never the same after their ducking, but my pride? No, sorry to disappoint you, but I can't say I suffered at all in that department. But I will say it stings a bit now to discover you think I'm the kind of cove who gets his jollies out of seeing the girl who gave him the heave-ho ruined. I always knew that your opinion of certain aspects of my character was pretty low, but do you really take me for a villain, Harry?"

"Yes. No, of course not. Confound it, Rawdon, you're only human. I haven't been exactly deaf, you know, to all the whispers behind my back. 'How the high and mighty have fallen' or words to that effect. You can well imagine what people have been saying."

"I doubt I could, Harry. For I could never have imagined what you just said."

"They're saying what a lucky escape you've had and what a fool I was to throw you over."

"And I take it you don't agree."

44

"Well, I'll grant you your lucky escape, of course. My dowry, along with the estate that should have marched with yours, went to the creditors when Papa died. But as for the other—being a pauper hasn't changed my outlook. I've no desire to share a husband with a gaggle of opera dancers or any other form of lightskirt."

He studied her thoughtfully, his face inscrutable. "Let's table that last bit for a moment, shall we? But since you've brought up the subject, how are you getting on, Harry?"

*"Harriet.* No, dammit, *Lady Harriet."*

"Not only independent but foulmouthed, too, I see. By God, *Lady* Harry, you'd have made a capital man."

"Well, at least I'd have known enough to avoid two of the vices of that sex—gambling and womanizing."

"Surely I'm only accused of one of those—and rather unjustly when it comes to that." He ignored her eloquent sniff. "But we weren't going to talk about that, remember? Just let me point out that you'd have been wasted as a man. Not that you aren't as a woman. At least I, for one, consider it a waste that you got more than your fair share of beauty. And, by the by, I always thought that you were at your very best in that riding habit."

"Don't try it on me, Rawdon. I'm quite immune to your flattery."

"You think I don't know that? I wouldn't waste my time."

"And speaking of wasting time." She started to rise, but he reached across and clasped her wrist. "Not so fast, Harry. You haven't answered my question yet. And as your oldest friend, I've a right to know."

"Friend!" she hooted.

"Yes, friend," he answered firmly. "I may have made a hash of it as a fiancé, but I was always a good friend, and you damn well know it. Now tell me. How are you getting on?"

"I keep body and soul alive."

"We've already discussed your body, and I'm not qualified to discuss your soul, so could you try to be a little more forthcoming?"

"I still see no reason—oh, very well then," she sighed and capitulated. "I own this cottage outright. Miss Kate stays with me merely for her board and keep. She takes care of the housekeeping and, with the help of a job man who comes to do the heavy work, I manage the garden."

"I've been sitting here admiring it. One of the prettiest I've ever seen." He gazed appreciatively at the flowerbeds alive with roses, pinks, and lilies of all shades and varieties.

"Yes, it is nice, isn't it." Her expression softened. "It sustains us. So you see, all in all, I don't do too badly. I've adjusted quite well, thank you."

"Aren't you leaving out the most important part, though?"

"What do you mean?"

"Why your new career, of course."

"Oh, you know about that, do you?" She was hostile once again.

"Any reason why I shouldn't?"

"Not especially. Only I don't wish to be ridiculed, that's all."

"Ridiculed! My God, here we go again. Why would I *ridicule* you?"

"Or patronized."

"Not that either. You're getting to be just a bit tiresome, Harry. Your pieces are damned good."

"How would you know that?"

"I've read 'em. Several of them, anyhow."

"You've read *Ladies' Magazine*?" She stared, incredulous. "How ever did you manage to see that particular periodical? No, on second thought, don't tell me. I don't think I wish to know."

"There you go again," he sighed. "I really wish I was half the success with the fair sex that you give me credit for."

She looked him up and down, uncomfortably aware of his attractiveness. "I expect you do all right," she observed dryly.

"Thank you. But as to how I saw your stuff, a number of my female relations—including Susan's mother, by the by—made sure I got copies. I rather suspect it's a feminine conspiracy to let me know you get along without me very well, thank you. But all the same, I actually enjoyed your pieces. I must say that your descriptions of country life really took me back. But I am surprised that you haven't been run out of Berkshire. Some of your character descriptions were down right libelous." He chuckled at the memory.

"Oh no, not really, I'm very careful never to write about real people. My characters are—well, composites, I guess you'd call them—of persons whom I've known."

"Fustian. If you didn't dish up our sexton to the world, then I'm a Dutchman." He reached for the pot and poured the dregs into his cup. "Oh I know you gave him gray hair and a lot of extra years and pounds, but that was still Ben Bass, don't deny it."

"Well, mostly," she admitted. "But you're one of the very few, I trust, who'd know that. And one thing's for sure, I've discovered that people never recognize themselves."

"Now there's a sobering thought. Are you saying that you've vilified me in one of those sketches and I never knew it?"

"I wouldn't waste my ink."

"Let's see," he mused. "There was a particularly unpleasant old bachelor. An ex-military cove, in fact. By George, I'll bet that was me."

She laughed. "Well, if it pleases you to think so."

"It doesn't in the least. The truth is, I rather fancied myself as the hero of that cricket match you once described."

"Don't be goosish. The man was a blacksmith."

"Well, you did say you changed bits here and there. And the cove won the day. Sounds just like the sort of thing I would do," he grinned.

"Trust me, Colonel, you have never appeared, nor will you ever appear, in any of my writings."

"So much for immortality." He gave an exaggerated sigh and then grew serious. "Tell me, Harry, do they pay you well?"

"That, sir, is none of your concern."

"Oh, hell, Harry, don't take that lofty tone with me. Just promise me one thing, will you? If you're ever in difficulty of any kind, come to me first. You do know, don't you, that I'm always good for a touch?"

She rose to her feet. "I really should be getting back to the Hall now. I told Mariana that I wouldn't be gone any longer than it took to check on things. I'm helping her with arrangements for the birthday ball."

48

"Well, I've made a botch of this, too," he sighed as he also stood.

"No, you haven't, Rawdon." She couldn't quite force herself to look at him. "I do appreciate the gesture on your part."

"Gesture?" he bristled.

"A poor choice of words. The offer, then. And I am grateful. Truly. It just isn't necessary, that's all."

He shrugged and dropped the subject. "Come on, then. I'll ride back with you."

"Must you?"

"Why ever not? Scared of the gossip mongers? After all that character assassination in your pieces, seems only fair to give the local folk a chance to get their own back."

Rawdon went to fetch their horses while Harriet had a word with her companion. Then, as she emerged through the glass doors, she froze in horror. "My God, what's that?" He followed her gaze, looking rather puzzled.

A sleek, glossy greyhound, pure white except for some black spotting upon her small head, was being chased round and round by a hideous, large galloping mongrel, the unhappy product of some mysterious melding of breeds, the only identifiable component being sheep dog. The mongrel caught up with the graceful bitch (due entirely to cooperation on her part), gave her a mock-ferocious nip, then wheeled and took off again at top speed with the greyhound in pursuit.

"Well," said the colonel, "it looks very much to me like two dogs playing. What did you take it for?"

Lady Harriet didn't answer. She was tearing through the garden after the dogs. "Christobel," she shouted, with a clap of her hands. "Come here!"

The greyhound ignored her.

"This minute, do you hear me?" She clapped her hands noisily again, in rapid fire.

Christobel, deaf by all appearances, effortlessly succeeded in tagging the mongrel, then ran off like an arrow shot from a bow.

"Christobel, come here!" her mistress shouted.

Colonel Melford had been ambling along behind her ladyship, taking an amused interest in the affair. He now put two fingers to his lips and whistled. The mongrel stopped dead in his tracks, gave the colonel a reproachful look, then came galloping to his side.

Lady Harriet had turned livid. "Is that creature yours?"

"Good doggie, Dolph." Rawdon was patting the shaggy head affectionately. "Well, yes, I suppose you might say so. Though it's been a rather loose association. He joined me some time back, and we've been keeping company ever since."

"Well, you keep him away from my bitch while you're here." Her voice was dangerous.

"Seems to me the injunction should work the other way," he observed as they were joined by Christobel who kept licking and nipping the big dog affectionately, trying to reinstigate the game. "You keep your bitch away from my Adolphus."

"I'll do that," she said between clenched teeth as she grabbed the greyhound by the collar, dragged her across the lawn, and shoved her through the door inside the house. The animal immediately began to scratch and howl her protest.

Colonel Melford tried, without a great deal of success, to keep a straight face as he helped Lady Harriet mount her horse. "The stupid bitch," she said as she glared at him. "She has no taste."

"Well that's the trouble with over-bred females, ain't it? They seldom know what's good for them."

The grin broke loose as Harriet gave her mare a kick and left him standing there.

# Chapter
# Seven

Absently, JEM SHAFTOE continued to brush imaginary specks from his master's evening-clad shoulders while the other eyed him speculatively in the glass. The colonel was seated at a dressing table putting his own final touches to his cravat. "I say there," he finally protested, "you'll have me threadbare if you keep that up."

"Sorry, sir." The valet snapped out of his reverie, put down the clothes brush and reached for the pomade. The colonel sighed and removed it from his hand. "You just did that, Jem. Want me to shine and smell like a Frenchman?"

"Oh, sorry, sir." The valet removed the cravat.

"For God's sake, Shaftoe!" the colonel exploded. "I really wish you'd get your mind on what you're doing."

"It's dead on target, sir. Oh I'll admit to woolgathering there for a bit or I'd have stopped you before you made such a botch of your starcher." He tossed the crumpled cravat to one side of the table and began to wind a fresh one about the colonel's neck.

"Do you realize, Jem," the other said conversationally, "that being in love's playing the very devil with your disposition?"

"Is that so, sir?" The valet stood back to squint critically in the glass at his own creation, the Melford fall.

"Damn right. You used to be a highly entertaining cove. I could count on you to dish out the dirt in any household where we were staying. Now you've scarcely said a word for the last half hour. I take it, then, that your suit ain't exactly prospering?"

The colonel got up from the dressing table and walked over to a chest of drawers where he pulled out two cigars. He tossed one to the valet. There was a moment's silence while the two men lighted up. "Well?" the colonel prodded when both cigars were puffing satisfactorily. "How is the wooing going?" He plopped down in a wing chair and waited.

Shaftoe sat on the dressing table stool and frowned at the cigar he was holding. "It's not," he sighed.

"You did go to the Magpie this afternoon, didn't you? Come on, man, out with it. What happened?"

"Not a lot. I didn't get much chance to talk to her."

"Her old man chaperoning, was he?"

"That too. But mostly, she had some toff in tow and was playing him off against the farmer and myself. Of course," he smiled dreamily at the recollection, "I did give the little flirt something to think about there in the barn before I left her."

"Why, you old dog, you!" The colonel looked at his valet with new respect. Then, after he'd wormed the entire story of Shaftoe's encounter with Miss Flack out of him, he said, "Tell me about the toff."

"Not much to tell. Except it's a bit of a mystery why he's hanging around here."

"The fair Rosina?"

The valet's face darkened. "That's one explanation. She's certainly leading him on for all she's worth. But like I said, I think that's mostly for the benefit of the farmer and me. The cove's a gentleman, you see, though not as much a one as he lets on, I'll wager. But he'll not be marrying the likes of Rosy Flack. And I'm thinking she's too flash by half to let herself be taken in. But then, when it comes to females, you never know. And he is a handsome devil—if you like the type."

"Tall is he?" Rawdon grinned.

"Go to the devil, sir." Shaftoe grinned back, then immediately looked thoughtful. "It's *Major* Mortram they call him. And I couldn't begin to tell you why, but somehow I don't think he is one."

"Don't look the part?"

"N-no," the other mused. "I'd say he looks it a bit too much."

"Hmmm. Well, cheer up. Maybe he'll move on in a day or so. Of course that still leaves the farmer." The colonel dropped cigar ash on the carpet as his valet winced. "What would you say his chances are?"

"Damned good. Old man Flack is pushing him for all he's worth, of course."

"Well sometimes that can backfire. Especially with a high-spirited girl like your Rosina. Bit of a clod besides, didn't you say?"

"A trifle thick, yes."

"Well, there you are. And young Rosina's nobody's fool. Sharp as a knife, I'd call her."

"True enough. But there's that farm. Which is bad enough. But I found out worse today. Holton's a cricket wizard."

"Is that so?" Colonel Melford looked impressed.

"Oh yes. He's the local hero in fact. And old Flack's cricket mad, as is everybody else in this benighted place—including little Rosina."

"Well, that's nothing to put you in a pucker. You're a dab hand yourself."

"Think they'll take my word for it?" the valet sighed. "By the by, the 'major' also claims to be an expert."

"Does he now? He gets more and more intriguing."

"But that's enough about my affairs, sir. How's your wooing going?"

The colonel, inhaling, choked on his cigar. "My what?"

"Your pursuit of Lady Harriet. How's it coming?"

"Now what the devil makes you think I'm pursuing Harry?"

"Why else would you put up with all of this?" A sweeping gesture took in the Fawcett household. "Why, to give you a chance to court Miss Flack, you widgeon."

"If you say so, sir."

"I do say so, dammit," the colonel glared, then grinned sheepishly under the valet's knowing eye. "All right, then, since you ask. Things aren't going at all well. The fact of the matter is, she doesn't appear to like me all that much."

"I don't believe that, sir. You've got to remember, Lady Harry's proud."

"Lord, don't I know it."

"And, well, not to put too fine a point on it, you did dash a bit of cold water on that pride."

"That's nothing to what she did to my satin knee smalls."

"And losing her fortune's bound to have been a blow. Made her even more prickly, I daresay."

"A regular hedgehog." The colonel grimaced. "You won't believe—" His thought was interrupted by the mantle clock striking six. "Oh Lord, here we go again. Time for dinner." He rose and snuffed his cigar in the china washbasin, an act which his valet viewed almost as dimly as strewing the Aubusson with ash. "You know, you may be right. I must be in love not to shake the dust of this place off my feet. You can't imagine the atmosphere at these cursed meals."

"Well, I can begin to. Servants' hall's a bit the same. Rather like two armed camps. Half of 'em, led by the cook, side with Lady Selina and feel that his lordship had no business marrying a child bride. The others, mostly younger, think her new ladyship's very nice and Lady Selina's being a brat." He looked the colonel over critically and flicked a bit of cigar ash off his lapel. "But, cheer up, sir. There'll be another guest here tonight. That could lessen hostilities a bit."

"Oh really, who?"

"A Mr. Evelyn Forbes. The local squire's son. He and Lady Selina used to play together as children, so I'm told. And it's the opinion in servants' hall that Lord Fawcett's setting out to do a little matchmaking. A sort of diversionary tactic, you might say."

"I certainly would say, since I'm the one who suggested the thing in the first place."

"I know, sir."

"You know? Just how the devil—Well, never mind. You always do know everything. And for God's sake, don't come at me with that damned clothes brush again."

The valet grinned as the door slammed in his face.

\* \* \*

Mr. Evelyn Forbes was an amiable young gentleman with an open countenance, brown hair, and pale blue eyes. Though he perhaps was not quite handsome, few people ever noticed that oversight. But if he was expected to restore harmony to the Fawcett dinner table, such a task soon proved well beyond his powers.

Lady Selina, seated beside him, appeared to suspect what her father was up to and was determined to nip those expectations in the bud. She repeatedly snubbed all her old friend's attempts at conversation. So after despairing of the boorish lady on his right, the young man turned to Lady Harriet on his left. She, however, was discussing coursing with her host. Mr. Forbes sighed inwardly and concentrated his attention on his roasted pigeon.

Lady Fawcett could sympathize with any victim of her stepdaughter's incivility. She came to the young man's rescue with a few inquiries that established a mutual interest. A spirited discussion of horse racing took place across Selina who seemed fascinated by the pattern of her dinner plate and sullenly rearranged her food in order to best see the forget-me-nots.

Lord Fawcett, whose conversation with Lady Harriet had progressed from coursing to greyhound breeding, became gradually aware of his wife's animated dialogue with a much younger man. He soon lost the thread of what he'd been saying and, like an unwound clock, ran down. Sir Rawdon tried to step into the breech and keep the subject going. His efforts only served to remind Lady Harriet that her stated plans for her prize thoroughbred could be easily overset by the colonel's mongrel. She glared indignantly at his expressed views on overbreeding.

He gave it up with a shrug and sipped his wine in silence.

Lady Fawcett, who suddenly realized that now everyone was listening to the anecdote she was telling Mr. Forbes, turned beet red and forgot the ending. She gave her frowning husband a timorous smile and joined the general silence. It came as a great relief to all the diners when at last the ladies left the gentlemen to their port.

Conversation among those remaining fared much better. They picked up on a topic dear to most male hearts. "What's all this I hear about a cricket match with the village?" the colonel asked, and the local gentlemen both brightened.

"It's a long-standing custom," Lord Fawcett explained. "The Hall always organizes an eleven to play the village team during the Maying."

"We never win, actually," Mr. Forbes added, a bit dampeningly.

"That's because they've got Joel Holton." His lordship expounded upon the farmer's cricket prowess while Rawdon pretended not to have heard it all before. "But we stand a jolly good chance of doing 'em in this time with you here," Fawcett beamed. He proceeded then, for the newcomer's benefit to give chapter and verse of the colonel's glory days on the playing field, while that gentleman endeavored to look modest. It was with some reluctance that the threesome finally dropped the subject and joined the ladies.

The social temperature of the drawing room did not rise above the dining room's frigid precedent. The hostess suggested cards. Selina demurred. Parlor games were pronounced childish. Finally, in desperation, Lady Fawcett went to the pianoforte and began to play, while suggesting that the others gather round and sing. Mr. Forbes alone responded to the invitation. He soon proved to have a remarkable tenor voice that blended most harmoniously with his hostess's sweet soprano. As a consequence of this pleasant discovery, the two musicians forgot all about the others and, alone of the group, quite enjoyed the remainder of the evening.

The young ladies retired to a sofa as far removed from everyone else as possible and spent their time in whispered consultation. Selina did seem rather inclined, however, to shoot surreptitious glances at the musical twosome more often than her desire for detachment seemed to warrant.

Lady Harriet, Colonel Melford, and their host were debating the relative merits of fox hunting and rabbit coursing. But Lord Fawcett's interest, like his daughter's, soon became more and more centered on the pianoforte, leaving the formerly affianced pair to carry on the discussion by themselves. Since neither saw a necessity for making small talk, the conversation lagged and finally ran down. At long last, when his wife showed no inclination to do so, his lordship took it upon himself to bring the musicale to an end by ringing for the tea board.

"I have, without a doubt, spent the dreariest evening of my entire life," Sir Rawdon informed his valet a bit later as Shaftoe helped him shrug out of his evening coat.

"A pity. But then 'the course of true love ne'er ran smooth,' sir."

"I do wish you'd pay attention, Jem. I'm talking

dismal, crushing boredom, and you're making up stupid platitudes that have nothing to say in the matter."

"Sorry, sir." Shaftoe, just managing to keep his face free of all expression, poured his master a stiff brandy and thrust it in his hand.

# Chapter
# Eight

SHAFTOE RETIRED TO his cot in the adjoining dressing room and was soon asleep. The colonel, clad in his nightshift, sat by an open window, gazing up rather dolefully at the darkened sky.

It was all of a piece, he decided, that this miserable evening couldn't even manage a supply of stars. He didn't ask for moonlight. But it did seem that a constellation or two to break the monotony was not too much to ask.

Rawdon sighed heavily and tossed off the dregs of his brandy. Maybe tomorrow would be a better day. Well, by Jove, he thought as an idea struck him and he reached for his brocade dressing gown, that was more or less up to him, now wasn't it?

The colonel made his way a bit unsteadily down the hall, pausing once to shield his sputtering candle with his hand as an errant breeze drifted up the corridor and threatened to extinguish it. He frowned at the row of doors in some perplexity. Preoccupation with the candle had caused him to lose count. And he was vaguely aware that he was slightly in his cups, a condition he was unaccustomed to coping with. Was this, then, the third door down? Wouldn't do to miscalculate. The very thought caused him to shudder. It was also a bit off-putting to detect no sign of light seeping out beneath the door. Oh well. He'd come this far. Nothing ventured, nothing gained. The colonel groped for the knob and turned it.

Lady Harriet had not been able to sleep either. She had opened the bed hangings as far as possible and removed her nightcap to take advantage of the bit of breeze that occasionally wafted through the casement windows. She had read until she finally felt drowsy enough to blow out her candle. But still she tossed and turned. She was just beginning to drift off at last when she was snapped back to full consciousness by the squeaking of a hinge.

Harriet sat bolt upright and peered through the darkness, straining to identify the creature invading her privacy in the dead of night. It progressed slowly to loom over her with its shrouded candle now extended before she found her voice and croaked, "Rawdon Melford! What the devil do you think you're up to? Ouch!" A glob of hot wax splattered on her foot. "Watch that candle, you blithering numbskull."

"Sorry," he mumbled, looking contrite.

"I realize," she whispered scathingly as she rubbed wax off her smarting toes, "that it's second nature for you to go wandering into ladies' boudoirs in the middle of the night, but this time you've picked the wrong one, you ninny."

"I have not," he countered, placing his candlestick on the night table and sitting down on the bed beside her. "I was worried there for a minute when my candle damn near went out that I'd become confused. But I got it in one." He beamed his triumph.

"I should have known. You're foxed."

"I am not! Well," he amended, "I may be a trifle castaway, but that has nothing to say to my being here. Fact is, I badly needed a restorative after the evening we just spent. I'm surprised you ain't drunk, Harry. You aren't, are you?" He sighed at the look she gave him. "Thought not. Not your style. Not usually mine, either, though I don't expect you to believe it. You always think the worst where I'm concerned, and that's the truth, Harry. But never mind all that. About this evening—I ask you, did you ever spend a worse evening in your life?"

"One, perhaps."

"Oh hell. We're back to that again. I vow, Harry, you can hold a grudge longer than anyone I've ever known." He gave her an injured look.

"Don't call me Harry. And if you're so miserable here, you can always leave, you know."

"No, I can't. I explained all that. Concerns Shaftoe. Didn't you listen?"

"All right then. But at least leave my room."

"Not till I do what I came here to do. Which, by the by, ain't at all what you were thinking." He was struck by a sudden thought. "That reminds me, what the devil did you mean by saying I'd picked the wrong room? That's downright slanderous. What other room would I have picked? The bride's, for God's sake? Well, I don't doubt that things between her and Fawcett are so bad that she could use some comfort, but I ain't the type to cuckold a friend in spite of what you think. Not in his own house, certainly," he amended. "And if you believe for one minute I'd give one of those two nubile juveniles the nod, you've got mice in your attic. Besides being unpleasant little baggages, one of 'em's me ward, which

63

sounds almost incestuous. So who does that leave, I ask you?"

"How would I know? There's bound to be a pretty parlor maid around here somewhere."

"It leaves you, that's who." The colonel looked quite pleased with this display of logic.

"Oh no, it doesn't. Get out of here, Rawdon, before I ring for someone to put you out."

"No need to be so hostile. I have no intention of trying to climb into your bed, if that's what you're hoping. All that you just said was a scurrilous libel. I do not make it a habit at house parties to search out females and spend the night. Now I do admit to having had a few of 'em search me out in my time." He chuckled wickedly.

"Rawdon, leave!"

"Not till I say what I've come for. Lady Harriet, will you go riding with me tomorrow?"

"No."

"Let's make it before breakfast. Not too early, though. Must be at least one or two o'clock by now. Oh I say, did you just say 'no'?"

"You heard me right."

"Why not, dammit? You're a bruising rider. Or used to be at any rate. You always liked to ride more than anything. And I couldn't help but notice there's no sign of a horse there at your place. So now I thought you'd leap at the chance. It's me, then, ain't it? You might as well go on and admit it, Harry. You don't want to ride with *me*."

"Oh, I wouldn't mind admitting it in the least. But since I've promised to help Mariana in the morning, there's no need to be offensive."

"Sounds like a pretty lame excuse to me. But that's all right." He slid off the bed and picked up his candle. "I'll take Shaftoe. Will work out better anyway. There're some things we need to see to. G'night, Harry."

"Good night, Rawdon." Despite herself, she had trouble keeping the laughter from her voice.

She needn't have struggled, though, to save her dignity; the colonel's attention was elsewhere as he slowly crossed the room. It was the mention of Shaftoe that had put his brain cells in a whirl. There was some association there he was searching for, that kept eluding him till the very moment when his hand was on the knob. "By Jove, that's it," he muttered triumphantly as the revelation struck. "The very ticket, b'gad."

He wheeled and strode purposely, if somewhat unsteadily, back across the room while Lady Harriet gaped in astonishment. He placed the candle down once more upon the table, climbed once more upon the bed, and enfolded Lady Harriet in his arms. She was a strong woman and fought fiercely to break free when he first began to kiss her. But she proved no match for the powerful man who held her tight and soon ceased to struggle. Whether her abject surrender was caused by a realization of the futility of that struggle, or from other causes entirely, remained forever a moot question in Lady Harriet's mind.

Then, after a long, breathless interval, Sir Rawdon released her of his own accord. He searched his foggy mind for several seconds before Shaftoe's speech that had so impressed him finally came to mind. "If you were trying to make me jealous," the colonel quoted, "it worked a fair treat, lass." Well satisfied with this exit line's effect upon his audience, he then retrieved his candle and left the room.

Lady Harriet stared openmouthed at the closing door. "He's stark, raving mad. A jibbering idiot," she muttered to herself.

Other residents of the Hall also had had difficulty settling for the evening. When Lord and Lady Fawcett retired to their bedchamber, the atmosphere was strained, to say the least. After her ladyship's maid had finally left the room, his lordship opened the first salvo. "There is very little point in inviting young Forbes here, Mariana, if you intend to keep monopolizing him."

His wife stopped in the middle of the hundred brushes she usually gave her hair and stared at him in the glass as he loomed over her. Two angry spots glowed in her cheeks, but her voice was low and under control. "I've not the slightest notion of what you are talking about, Aubrey."

"I'm talking about you making young Forbes one of your flirts, and you dashed well know it. The poor mooncalf's down right besotted."

"You're the one who's besotted, I collect." She stared pointedly at the brandy in his hand. He, like the colonel, had sought an anodyne for the trying evening they'd just spent. "I was merely being civil to a guest. Heaven knows, someone had to be."

"Yes, by gad, *someone*, but not you. The whole point of the exercise, in case you've forgotten was to fling him at Selina's head. *She* was the one to be civil to him, not you."

"It may have escaped your lordship's notice," she retorted, "but your daughter is incapable of civility."

"Now see here, Mariana," he barked.

"No, sir, you see here!" She raised her voice in turn. Though dimly aware she was beginning to sound like a fishwife, Mariana didn't care. She was by nature sweet dispositioned, but the strain of the last several days had begun to take its toll. She reveled in the astonishment on her husband's face. "Your daughter, sir, is a spoiled, selfish brat who has no consideration for anyone else's feelings. I only did what any other hostess would have done when she froze out Mr. Forbes. I tried to make him feel welcome."

"Oh, you did that all right. You did it to a fair turn, you did. In fact, I could go so far as to say you overdid it."

"Well, if that's so—which I don't believe for one minute—it's because I, too, have been the victim of Lady Selina's frosty atmospheres and am prodigiously sympathetic with any other sufferer."

"And the fact that the so-called victim is young and handsome has nothing to say in the matter, I collect."

They were at daggers drawn indeed now, in this their very first quarrel. Both kept feeling a need to draw back, become conciliatory, but neither was capable of such action.

"Indeed, sir, I should try and make any guest feel comfortable. As for the motives you accuse me of, I do not consider Mr. Forbes particularly handsome. And only you would consider being young a crime."

"That's right," he said between clenched teeth, "they told me that if I robbed the cradle I could expect to wind up a cuckold."

"How dare you, sir!" For a moment they both believed she was going to throw the hairbrush at him. With a struggle she restrained herself.

"Don't call me 'sir'," he said wearily, all the anger draining away, leaving him merely tired.

"Why not? You insist upon seeing yourself as an ancient when you are merely forty."

"Not yet."

"In a week's time, then. Though what that has to say to anything is quite beyond me. Our ages were never at issue until your daughter made you prickly on the subject."

"Prickly? Me, prickly? Don't be absurd. And I do wish you'd try to get along with Selina."

She also had begun to simmer down, but was immediately put back on the boil again. "You wish *I'd* try and get along! You're lecturing the wrong person, sir. I have been all civility. It's your harpy of a daughter who needs the scold."

"Now just one minute, Mariana. I won't have you speaking this way of Selina. I know she can be difficult at times, but, dammit, she's me own flesh and blood."

"Then you should have taught her manners. Or perhaps civility was never valued in your family."

"In my family! How about your family?" His lordship, too, had found a second wind. "Don't lecture me on manners, Mariana. What about that rackety brother of yours, eh? He was supposed to have been here two days ago. And not only has he failed to show up, but he invited a guest here on his own initiative, then leaves it up to me to entertain the fellow. Don't talk to me about your family's refinement, for I won't have it. And I'll tell you something else, Mariana. If you've any notion of promoting a match here, well you can jolly well forget it. I'll not allow Selina to marry a here-and-therein like Soame Townshend."

"You won't what?"

"You heard me."

"As if *I'd* allow it. Why I'd sooner see him wed one of Macbeth's witches. Not that I need worry. He wouldn't look twice at your Selina."

"Oh no?" he sneered. "It's wonderful what some folk will do for a fortune."

He might as well have slapped her. She had turned quite pale. "And just what is that supposed to mean?" she asked quietly.

"Just that Soame is always behind with the world," he blustered, "and Selina is an heiress after all."

"In spite of what you seem to think, sir, my family is not in the habit of marrying for money. Now if you will excuse me, this has been a long and trying day, and I need my rest. Would you mind very much sleeping in your dressing room? I seem to be developing the headache."

"Not at all," he replied with the same exaggerated politeness. "In fact, I'd welcome it."

# Chapter
# Nine

WHEN THEY PASSED one another on the stairs the following morning, it was difficult to say which gentleman looked the worse for wear. The honors probably went to Lord Fawcett since Colonel Melford had by then consumed several cups of coffee to remedy some of the ill effects of too much brandy and very little sleep. He had, in point of fact, managed to take the stairs two at a time, which earned him a rather jaundiced look from his lordship.

After an almost grumpy "good morning," Fawcett, noting his guest's top boots, forced himself to do the civil. "Planning to ride then, are you? Nice morning for it." Actually, the bright sunlight through the windows was doing very little for his lordship's headache, but that was beside the point.

"Capital." The colonel, whose reaction to the glare was similar to his host's, sounded overhearty. "Oh I say, do you mind furnishing my valet with a mount?"

"Your valet's riding with you?" His lordship could not possibly have heard right.

"Yes. That is, if you've a horse to spare."

"Ain't that a bit unusual? Most coves would take their grooms."

70

"That's true. But then, Shaftoe's not your usual valet."

"Still, I never heard of such a thing. If you don't wish to ride alone, take my groom with you."

"No, no. You don't understand. Riding ain't the point. Except to get to a field I spotted. It's a bit far to walk it. Though of course we can do it if you'd rather."

After a quarrel with his bride and a night spent in his dressing room, Lord Fawcett was finding this a bit too much. "You wish to visit one of my fields? Whatever for?"

"Batting practice." The other lowered his voice conspiratorially. "That's why I'm taking Shaftoe. Need him to bowl for me."

"Your valet plays cricket?" Lord Fawcett shook his head to clear it, then winced from the pain this ill-advised maneuver caused him.

"Told you he wasn't your run-of-the-mill type. I'd like to practice away from the Hall, you see." The colonel looked around to be sure no servants were within earshot. "Since the village team is the big favorite, I'd rather it wasn't known that we're taking this business seriously. The odds against us should be pretty high, I'd say. As things stand, any cove that backs us should be able to win a bundle. So I'd rather not be observed. It could mess up the punting."

"By Jove, you're right." Lord Fawcett was brightening considerably. "But are you sure your valet's up to this sort of thing? You could take Forbes along." (Lord Fawcett just managed to say the name without rancor.) "He's a fair player," he conceded. "I'd offer to go myself, old man, but the truth is, I've got the devil's own headache."

"No, no. Thanks all the same. Shaftoe will do me fine."

"But a valet?" Lord Fawcett shook his head once more, to his sorrow, and they parted on the stairs.

The day was fine, with a few clouds scattered here and there to break the sky's monotony. And the field the colonel had chosen proved ideal, both level and secluded. "Of course it's really no matter if we're noticed," he observed as they set up makeshift wickets. "They'll just think you're practicing me."

"Well ain't I? Lord Fawcett's already got his team together, so I understand. And even if he hadn't, he'd not use me. It's a gentleman's eleven, remember?"

"Oh, I remember that. But you have to remember, 'when needs must, the devil drives.' "

"Sir?" The valet straightened up from placing a ball on the stumps to stare at his employer.

" 'When needs must, the devil drives,' " the gentleman repeated.

"And what the deuce is that supposed to mean? Sir."

"Damned if I know. It's just something people always seem to say in similar situations. To put it a bit more plainly then, don't worry your pretty head about making his lordship's team, Jem. Just leave it up to me."

"It seems a pretty daft idea, sir, if you don't mind my saying so. Wouldn't it make more sense for me to play for the village? That is, always supposing it makes sense to play at all."

"Now that," the other answered as he picked up the bat and gave it a few practice swings, "just serves to illustrate why I was a colonel and you a lowly sergeant."

72

"Oh?" The valet's eyebrows rose. "Well, I'm right glad to have that point cleared up, sir. Here I was thinking it had something to do with birth and the blunt to purchase a commission."

"That, too," the other conceded with a grin. "But the point is, me lad, that whereas you're a rare one in a fight, you ain't at all accustomed to plotting tactics. It's not enough, don't you see, to simply demonstrate your cricket ability to the fair Rosina. You've got to rub the farmer's nose in it. Not to mention the landlord's. In other words, you've got to beat the bastards. Now come on, bowl!" There followed an intense two hours of practice.

"Well, I won't say you ain't a bity rusty," the colonel remarked as they returned to Fairoaks. They were riding down a wide, green lane, lined on either side by oaks and beeches. Above their heads, thick branches formed an arbor where squirrels leaped from limb to limb and startled rooks took to the air to wheel and circle noisily. The two men were drained by their exercise, content to plod along. "No, you're not quite up to form yet, but nothing to worry about. A few more sessions like today's should do the trick. All in all, I'd say you play pretty well, Jem," he paused and hid a smile, "for a valet."

"That's generously said, sir, considering I bowled you out, let's see—twice?—three times, was it?"

"Once, and you damn well know it. And you were dashed lucky—oh I say, did you just see what I think I did?"

They had reached the rim of a winding valley, dissected by a small stream that guaranteed an emerald green turf even in the driest summer. Through the trees, the colonel had caught a glimpse of a man and woman standing on the bank holding hands. At

73

the sound of horses' hooves, they had quickly moved behind a clump of bushes. " 'Started like a guilty thing,' wouldn't you say?" Rawdon observed as he and Shaftoe continued on at an even slower pace. "It's impossible to be dead sure at this distance, but if that ain't my ward down there, I'll eat my hat. But who the devil's the cove with her?"

"Unless I'm much mistaken, that's the fellow Rosina was flirting with at the Magpie. I told you about him, sir, remember?"

"Oh yes, the questionable major. Mortlock you said his name was, didn't you?"

"Mortram," the valet corrected. "Brent Mortram."

"Heartbreaker type?"

"Most definitely. Females would flock like flies, I'm sure." Shaftoe scowled, recalling Miss Flack's absorption.

"Well, well, well. That certainly explains a lot, doesn't it? Why Susan thinks her mama sent me to spy on her, for one thing?"

"And why the 'major' is playing tourist in these parts."

"And why Susan dropped her victuals at the sight of me. Well, should we ride down and confront 'em? I am her guardian, after all."

"I'm not sure that's such a good idea, sir," the valet replied thoughtfully. "It would just serve to get the young lady's back up, most likely."

"Hmmm. I collect that's what her mother's done already. Probably just made the major seem all the more attractive. Forbidden fruit. That sort of thing."

"Exactly. It seems to me that discretion's the better part of valor here."

"And what's that supposed to mean?"

"I don't know precisely, sir. But the same people

who say 'needs must when the devil drives' came up with it. But it does appear to me," he continued more seriously, "that you might do better just to keep an eye on the situation and find out a little more about the major, rather than have a head-on confrontation with Miss Tunstall."

"You're probably right. Bad habit of yours, Jem. Very well then. I'll pretend I never saw a thing. Though I must admit I'd rather box the little baggage's ears."

"You sound downright parental, sir, if I may say so."

The colonel looked taken aback. "Do I, by gad. Hmmm. Well now, did you ever stop to think, Shaftoe, that if Lady Harriet hadn't cried off, I could have a child of my own now?"

"You're much too modest, Colonel. Eight years ago? Five or six, more likely."

"By Jove, you're right." Sir Rawdon lapsed into silence as he dealt with this sobering thought.

They were approaching Lord Fawcett's extensive park before either spoke again. "Well, would you look at that!" the valet breathed.

The colonel snapped out of his reverie, expecting to spy another trysting couple. "By Jupiter, this place is becoming deuced populated," was his comment. "Was this lot here before?"

"Don't think so." They reined in their mounts to take a better look.

The long, narrow valley had ended in a little green, sheltered on one side by the high, mossy stone wall that bordered the park and on another by a coppice. A tent was pitched up against the wall where overhanging oak boughs shaded it.

The area had been abuzz with activity. It stopped

abruptly once the horsemen were sighted. A tall, lean, Spanish-looking man stood before the tent flap staring their way. Three ragged urchins froze in the process of gathering sticks. The two mongrels with them also became motionless, not even barking. A donkey ceased cropping grass to look. A pretty, dark-eyed young woman stood poised by the brook with the pail she'd just filled balanced on her shoulder. The only exception to this frozen tableau was an old crone dressed in a tattered black cloak and bonnet. Bent over a three-legged iron kettle that testified to decades of blackening even before it encountered the smoke now curling round it, she never ceased her stirring. Her face was hidden from the horsemen, but they didn't doubt her scrutiny for a minute.

"Gypsies," the colonel commented as they clucked at their horses. "Wonder if Fawcett's given 'em permission to camp here."

"He'd not be that big a fool. Begging your pardon, sir. They'll poach him blind, I'm thinking."

"Hmmm. You're sure of that?"

"Bound to. Second nature, ain't it?"

"Well, yes. The only thing is, it's odd they'd be so open with their encampment. This ain't exactly the high road, but quite a few people do pass this way. And there are plenty of places they could have picked if they didn't wish to be seen, as Miss Susan and her major could testify, plague take 'em. But that lot back there seemed almost advertising their presence."

"You'd best tell his lordship about them, sir. His gamekeeper should be alerted."

"I'll do that," the colonel replied absently, his mind on other matters.

They let themselves through a park gate and had

ridden on for half a mile, with the colonel deep in thought, when he suddenly began to chuckle.

"Sir?"

"Tell me, Shaftoe, just what is it that gypsies are most noted for?"

"Poaching, like I said before."

"Besides that?"

"Well, some of 'em do tinkering. But if you ask me, that's mostly just a cover for their thieving."

"Yes, but that's still not what gypsies are famous for the whole world over." The colonel wheeled his horse around abruptly. "You go on to the Hall, Jem. I'll be along after a bit. Oh by the by, I think I dropped a bit of gravy on my coat last night at dinner."

"I've already sponged it, sir."

"Sorry. No need to sound insulted. I didn't mean to cast aspersions on your professionalism. See you by and by."

"And may I ask what you're up to, sir?" the valet called after him as he spurred away.

"I'm not up to anything," the colonel grinned back across his shoulder. "I'm simply going to get my fortune told."

# Chapter
# Ten

"GYPSIES HERE? THAT'S odd. We don't usually get them in these parts." Lord Fawcett was in his library. He had been staring moodily at a copy of *Waverly*, without really seeing it, before the colonel had interrupted this pursuit. "Folk around here are too careful of their possessions to make it worth their while, I collect. Still, I'd better tell the bailiff to keep his weather eye out."

"You do that." Sir Rawdon joined his host at the library table in the center of the book-lined room. "But I don't think there's really a lot to worry about. I think they're mainly here for other reasons. There's an old crone with 'em who's pretty famous as a fortune-teller."

"Fortune-teller!" Fawcett snorted. "Bunch of nonsense is more like it."

"Oh I agree. But this woman's an artist. I'll give her that. I watched her in action, and I don't mind saying I was quite impressed."

"Were you, by Jove?" His lordship carefully placed a leather bookmark on page one of *Waverly*. "Wouldn't have thought a thing like that was in your line of country."

"It ain't in the normal way of things. But it was downright uncanny the things she told a young couple who'd come to see her. At least that's what they said."

"I still can't believe you'd be taken in by all that mumbo jumbo."

"Oh I'm not a believer, if that's what you're thinking. But the thing is, you see, I found her dashed entertaining. So I took the liberty of inviting her to the Hall tonight to tell everybody's fortune. That is, if you have no objection, Fawcett. I told her I'd send word not to come if it doesn't suit. Otherwise, she'll be here after dark."

"Well, now, I don't know," his lordship frowned. "Don't like the notion of having one of the thieving creatures loose in my house."

"Oh I don't think there's much to worry about. There'll be too many of us around."

"Yes, but she'll be able to look over the place for a return trip."

"That's possible, of course," the colonel admitted. "But with the army of servants you've got here, it wouldn't be a practical proposition. Besides, I'm paying her enough to keep temptation at bay."

"Oh I wouldn't allow you to do that, old boy." Lord Fawcett was weakening.

"But I insist. It's my idea entirely."

"Well, I must agree that it does sound diverting. And, frankly, anything would be an improvement over last night."

The colonel tactfully bit back his hearty agreement. "So it's settled then?" He rose to his feet. "Oh, just one other thing, Fawcett. I'd rather you didn't say I arranged this."

"Why ever not?"

"Well it won't be any fun unless everybody goes along. And, well, I seem to have put Miss Tunstall's back up, as you may have noticed."

"Now that you mention it, she does tend to treat you like a pariah. But since the whole damn household is at sixes and sevens, it's scarcely made an impression."

Again, the colonel thought it best not to comment on that particular point and reverted to their original topic. "It occurred to me, you see, that in the normal way of things, it's the young ladies who are the most likely to enjoy having their fortunes told. But if Miss Tunstall thinks it's all my idea, she's unlikely to go along. And if she doesn't, your daughter won't, and, well, the evening's ruined."

"Hmmm. See what you mean. All right then, I won't mention your name at all."

After a bit of small talk and cigars, the colonel left to change out of his riding clothes, and Lord Fawcett went to find his bailiff. As he crossed the hall his lordship became conscious of a repeated clicking sound that reminded him of his hostly duty. He peered round the door of the billiard room and confirmed what he'd suspected. He then strode purposefully off to find his daughter.

He discovered her in the morning room, seated by the window, studiously working on a pastoral scene in colored silks. "Where's Miss Tunstall?" he asked abruptly, but failed to notice it when his daughter's face turned pale.

"She's . . . uh . . . resting."

"Good. That leaves you free to entertain young Forbes."

"Me?" Her face set stubbornly. "Why should I entertain him?"

"Because he's a guest in this house, and he's on his own, that's why."

"Well," she tossed her head, "I certainly didn't invite him."

"No, dammit, I did," her father erupted. "And all because I thought he'd be good company for you and your friend. I wasn't to know that your ill nature would be directed at the whole world, now was I? I thought it was especially reserved for Mariana and me. Well, like it or not, Miss, I'm making young Forbes your responsibility. He's in the billiard room. Now you go do the civil."

There was something in her father's look and tone that made Selina think twice about further protest. This was a side of her indulgent parent she'd not seen before. She laid aside her tambouring and went.

Evelyn Forbes was leaning over the billiard table, cue in hand, studying the distribution of the balls through narrowed eyes. He raised up as Lady Selina came into the room. The look he bent upon her was not warm and friendly. "Looking for someone?" he inquired icily.

"You."

"Really? Whatever for?" He put down his cue stick and folded his arms. "Not for the pleasure of my company, I'll wager."

"My father thinks you're being neglected."

"Sooner neglected than given the leper treatment. That's it, by George. You've fetched me a bell."

"Your sense of humor leaves a lot to be desired, Mr. Forbes."

"So do your manners, Lady Selina. By the by, where's your equally disagreeable friend?"

"If you're referring to Miss Tunstall, she has the headache. She's resting."

"Well, now, normally I could believe that well enough, for the atmosphere of this place is enough to give anybody the headache. But the thing is, I saw her ride out of here some time ago. And by herself. Deuced odd, I thought it."

"How dare you spy on my friend," she glared.

"Spy! If you call glancing out my bedchamber window spying, well then I'm guilty." He perched on the edge of the table. "And I'll also confess to a bit of curiosity. What the devil are you two up to with your heads together all the time and now this talk of spying?"

"Don't be absurd. We're not 'up to' anything. I just resent you prying into my guest's privacy, that's all."

"Well if that's your attitude, then you'd better know that I couldn't care less about your little fits and starts. If you say so, I'm quite willing even to believe that a good jolting on horseback is the best remedy for the headache." He picked up a cue and tossed it to her. "Here. Let's have a game. You used to be pretty good at this when we were children."

"Billiards is not a proper game for ladies."

"Oh, is that what they taught you at Madame St. Quintin's boarding school? And here I thought they'd only made you insufferable. Didn't notice they'd turned you into a lady, too. Or are those two things one and the same in your eyes?"

"*You* call *me* insufferable? Of all the nerve!" She picked up a cue stick. "And just how would you term

82

your own behavior, pray tell? You—you—dog in the manger!"

"Now just what the devil's that supposed to mean?"

"You know perfectly well."

"The deuce I do. What reasonable man could keep up with your crochets? I fail to see what dogs and mangers have to do with me."

"Just that it's pretty dog-in-the-mangerish to make your host's wife one of your flirts, that's all."

"One of my whats?" His face flushed with anger.

"You heard me." They were ten years old again, holding their cue sticks like quarterstaves.

"I was hoping I hadn't. For of all the shabby accusations, that one has to take the prize. Good God, Selina, I'd realized that you were jealous, but I didn't know you were a lunatic as well."

"Jealous? Jealous? Of you? And you have the gall to call *me* a lunatic!"

"Not of me, you nodcock. It's Mariana you're jealous of."

"*Mariana! Mariana!* You're on a first name basis? I must say, sir, that you—or she—waste no time."

"And why shouldn't I call her Mariana? I call you Selina, don't I?"

"Yes," she pounced, "but do you call my father Aubrey?"

"Of course I don't. It ain't the same thing at all."

"And why ever not?"

Too late, he saw the trap she'd led him into. "You don't first-name a cove who bounced you on his knee when you were in leading strings," he answered sullenly.

"Why don't you just go on and say it. Papa's an

83

ancient, and she's your age. And I am not jealous of her. At least not in the way you mean. What I do resent is the fact that she's made such a complete cake out of Papa. The whole neighborhood's laughing at him. As you well know."

"I know no such thing. If anything, the whole neighborhood—with the exception of the usual old tabby cats—wishes him well. Most think he married a very nice lady. And," he challenged her with a look, "a beauty."

"It's easy to see that she's got you wrapped around her finger," Selina retorted. "Well, she's simply playing you off against Papa. And it's working. He's in a regular rage. And why else would he be throwing me at your head? I'm supposed to divert you from Mariana."

"W-what?" he choked. "Think you're up to the weight?" His smile was meant to irritate. "I'd personally say your stepmama's got you outclassed, and that's why your nose is so out of joint."

"And I think we'd better play," she said between tight lips, "before I forget what these sticks were really intended for."

She drove her cue ball viciously against the far end cushion. He followed suit, his ball rebounding slightly nearer.

"I've got you there, but never mind. Ladies first." He bowed with mock gallantry.

"Don't do me any favors," she glared back.

The contest that ensued was intense and silent, each one attacking the ball as if actually seeing the other's head. At the battle's conclusion, he crowed in triumph. "Fifty points! My game, your ladyship."

"Go to the devil, Evelyn." She flung her cue down

84

on the green felt surface and strode angrily toward the door.

"Tsk, tsk!" he clucked after her. "Such unsportswomanlike conduct. What would Madame St. Quintin say?"

He chuckled wickedly as she slammed the door behind her.

# Chapter
# Eleven

LORD FAWCETT'S ANNOUNCEMENT that a gypsy fortune-teller would be there any moment certainly got everyone's attention. The gentlemen had just rejoined the ladies after a dinner only slightly less strained than the previous evening's. Though the reaction to his lordship's news was varied, everyone's interest was definitely piqued. The interval of waiting was used to exchange tales they'd heard of the accuracy of such predictions. These accounts were met with cynical skepticism or wide-eyed acceptance, depending on the disposition of the listener.

"I think it's all a bunch of rubbish," Mr. Forbes declared.

"Do you indeed?" The colonel's eyebrows rose.

"Don't tell me you believe in that mumbo jumbo. I'll not credit it."

"Well," the colonel said, quite seriously, "I used to feel the same way you do. But there was this Spanish gypsy—when I was in the Peninsula, you know. Well, let's just call me agnostic, for after that experience I can no longer disbelieve."

Miss Tunstall's, Lady Selina's, and Lady Fawcett's eyes grew wide. Lady Harriet's, however, narrowed as she regarded her ex-fiancé suspiciously.

"The Romany person has arrived, your lordship." Catley's disapproving countenance left little doubt as to which side of the issue he favored.

"Well, now then, ladies first," Lord Fawcett directed after the butler had withdrawn. But this met with considerable opposition. The majority of the ladies were apprehensive.

"Why don't you go, Harry?" Colonel Melford prodded. "Don't tell me you're scared. I'll not believe it."

"Let's just say then that I don't wish to have the gypsy practice on me. I'd like her to be well warmed up and in her stride before she reads my palm. Why don't you go first? You seem to be the only one of us experienced in these things."

"Very well then, I will." Sir Rawdon tried not to appear too eager. "That is if you're sure I'm not preempting one of you ladies." He peered round the group but got no volunteers. "Oh all right then, here I go."

At first, Colonel Melford felt he'd made a big mistake by taking the gypsy woman out of her element. She had looked far more authentic stirring her blackened pot, with the tent, the donkey cart, and the out-of-doors for atmosphere, than she did among the riotous Rococo plaster work of the hall, which was as far as Catley dared admit her. What's more, she was still wearing the same old grubby black bonnet and ragged cape. She could at least have donned bright scarves and shawls and golden earrings for her readings, he thought crossly. And yes, by gad, she smelled. He greatly feared that no one would take her seriously.

The gypsy's black-currant eyes were fixed on him

knowingly. "Sit down," she said in a heavily accented voice, nodding to the small tapestried chair she'd drawn up in front of her, a duplicate of the one she sat in.

"I say," the colonel remained standing and looked about the hall disapprovingly. "This really won't do, will it?"

"What exactly troubles you about the room, Colonel Melford?"

"Everything. It's much too large. And all these alcoves with busts and urns—and the crystal chandelier—the staircase. There's no atmosphere. It's all too—too—ordinary."

The old crone's eyes traveled about her, taking in the grandeur. "You are fortunate indeed, Colonel," she said dryly, "to find this ordinary."

"You know what I mean, confound it. The fortune-teller I went to in Spain had all sorts of trappings—crystal balls, zodiac signs, incense. You know the sort of thing. And it was so dark you could hardly see her. Mysterious, don't you know."

"I read palms, Colonel. And I'm almost seventy-five years old. I need light to see the lines properly. Now then, we're wasting time." She gestured impatiently at the chair. "Besides the gentry, I'm to give the servants readings. And I've no desire to be here all night. Let's get on with this."

"I'm not here to get my fortune told," the colonel blustered. "I just want to make sure you remember all I've told you about these people. The most important thing, of course, is for you to put the fear of God into Miss Tunstall. Warn her off that cove she's meeting on the sly."

"I remember your instructions precisely, Colonel."

88

"Good."

"But you're mistaken if you think I have the power to alter destiny."

"Well, you can at least put a flea in destiny's ear, can't you? Do your best. I'll go send the next one to you."

"Not till I look into your palm." The old Crone's eyes impaled him.

"I said that's not necessary. You'll get paid all the same."

"And just what are you afraid of, Colonel?"

"Oh the devil with it." Rawdon plopped down in the chair to its peril and stuck out his upturned hand. "Get on with it then, will you?"

Afterwards, the colonel was looking a bit chastened as he went back upstairs to direct the others to the gypsy, one by one.

When the fortune-teller had finished reading their palms and had gone on to the servants' hall, the house party gathered round the tea board. "Well now," his lordship said heartily, trying to instill some party atmosphere into his subdued and thoughtful guests, "let's all share what the gypsy told us."

"But we mustn't tell," his daughter protested, "or it won't come true."

"That's wishes, peagoose," Mr. Forbes said witheringly. "Of course we can tell what the old witch said. How else will we ever discover that it's all a bunch of moonshine? Now take you, for instance, Selina. Since you're so worried about breaking the spell, I'll bet a monkey she said you're going to marry a handsome prince, Cinderella."

"Something like that."

"How did they ever come up with all those handsome princes in all those stories anyhow?" Lady Fawcett wondered aloud. "Take our Prinny, for example. My brother says he's so grossly fat he's hideous and his corsets creak."

"I understand he fit the role when he was young, though," Lady Harriet offered.

"I say, let's not change the subject here," Evelyn Forbes protested. "I want to know what the old hag told Selina."

"What possible concern is it of yours?" If he thought for one minute she was going to confide that the gypsy had predicted she'd marry the first lad who'd ever kissed her, well he was much mistaken.

"We all said we'd tell, didn't we? Otherwise, what's the point?"

"He's right, you know." Lord Fawcett intervened in what appeared to be blowing into a squabble. "I thought it could be quite entertaining. Of course we all realize it's a bunch of nonsense. That's what makes it amusing. So why don't we go around the circle here. I don't mind starting. The gypsy told me I'd have a son."

"Oh did she, Aubrey?" His wife turned a glowing face toward him. "That's exactly what she said to me."

"Well, I should certainly hope so," the colonel remarked, sotto voce, and everybody, with the exception of Selina, laughed.

"What else did she tell you, m'dear?" For the first time in a long while, Lord Fawcett was looking tenderly at his bride.

"Oh that was just about it," she fibbed. She certainly wasn't going to admit that her palm had betrayed her deep unhappiness. Or that the gypsy had predicted that the person troubling her life would have a change of heart. "Oh yes, she did say that someone I love is very near."

"Well, I should certainly hope so." Lord Fawcett imitated the colonel's tone and once more there was laughter. "What about you, Harriet?" he asked.

"Well, you'll all be pleased to know that I shall shortly come into a fortune. Though not half so pleased as I am, I can assure you."

"Congratulations," Evelyn said seriously, bringing on more chuckles.

"Well?" the colonel prodded.

"Well what?" Lady Harriet countered.

"Surely that can't be all she told you."

"Believe me, in my strained circumstances, it will suffice. But were you expecting more?" Her dark eyes seemed to have taken on the gypsy's knack of seeing through him.

The colonel squirmed a bit uncomfortably. "Just wondered. Seems like you were in there a deuced long time to hear so little, that's all."

"Oh very well then, if you insist. There was the usual nonsense about a handsome stranger coming into my life."

He strangled on his tea. "A stranger!" he sputtered when he'd recovered. Either she was making the whole thing up or he'd get a refund from that old hag.

"A *handsome* stranger. Tall. Red-haired. Light eyes—the gypsy couldn't decide between gray and blue. Anyhow, I'm afraid I didn't take that part very seriously. But the part about the fortune, that I believe," she chuckled. "Now it's your turn, Evelyn."

"Well—she said there wouldn't be a lot of excitement in my life."

"When was there ever?" Selina jeered.

"But she also said I'd find great contentment," he bristled. "What's so bad about that, your ladyship?"

"Not a thing if you're attuned to dull. What else, pray?"

"She said I'd marry someone sweet and loving. God knows I've wracked my brain over that one and damned if I can come up with a soul that fits the description."

"Rosina Flack at the Magpie, perhaps? I've heard you've been spending a lot of time there of late, and that she's most sweet and loving to you. Or to anybody else in trousers, when it comes to that."

"Selina, that will do!" her father barked. "What about you, Rawdon?" He turned to the colonel, who was eyeing young Forbes askance as a possible new rival for Jem Shaftoe. "What did the fortune-teller say to you?"

"Eh what? To me? Oh yes, let's see. Well, for one thing, she said I'd soon be legshackled and would have three children."

"Are you sure she didn't say *mistresses*?" Lady Harriet asked sweetly.

"*Children.* And she also said I'd be a true and faithful husband who would fill my spouse's life with great happiness." His haughty stare dared his ex-fianceé to challenge this.

She contented herself with a derisive sniff. "Let's hear from you, Selina."

"Well, I'm to cross waters," Selina offered.

"The mill pond, maybe?" Evelyn asked.

"The channel, I expect. At any rate, I'm to marry

a noble foreigner," she wound up unconvincingly. "It's your turn, Susan."

Since her encounter with the gypsy, Miss Tunstall had been in a daze, scarcely hearing what anybody said, only rousing herself to join in, synthetically, with the general laughter. The truth was, she'd been quite shaken by the old woman's warning: there was a sinister man in her life that could bring about her ruin. He was a liar and a cheat. He did not love her. He loved her fortune.

Well, she didn't know how the old fake had come up with her information, but of course she didn't believe a word of it. Everyone of sense knew that fortune-tellers were charlatans.

"Come, on, Susan, tell us what the gypsy told you," her friend Selina was prodding. Susan searched her mind for anything she could say aloud. There had been more. Some nonsense the old hag had tagged on at the end. Oh yes, she now remembered. She looked around the circle and smiled shakily. "The gypsy said I'd see the man I'm going to marry this very evening and that he'd be wearing a pink waistcoat."

"Pink! My word!" Evelyn hooted. "Sounds a bit missish for my tastes. And there's certainly nothing of that description here." He gazed around him. All waistcoats were uniformly white beneath severe black, long-tailed evening coats. "Looks like you're out of luck. So much for—"

Whatever he might have planned to say was suddenly preempted by the sounds of swiftly approaching footsteps. The drawing room door burst open, and Mr. Soame Townshend came striding into the room. He went directly to the circle of chairs and stooped to kiss his sister on the cheek. "I beg pardon for arriving at such an hour and several days late at that, but I got tied up in the metropolis, don't you know."

His engaging, apologetic smile was meant to encompass the entire group. But no one saw it. All eyes were riveted upon his waistcoat.

# Chapter
# Twelve

"So I'm DESTINED to marry this young lady, am I?"
Mr. Soame Townshend smiled Miss Susan Tunstall's
way and she colored prettily.

He was a nice-looking young man, bearing a family resemblance to his sister. His eyes were the same
intense blue, though his hair was darker. He was of
medium height and build and something of a dandy.
"I do hope you're an heiress, Miss Tunstall, for I
haven't a feather to fly with."

"Oh she is," Lady Selina blurted, then could have
sunk under her father's disapproving stare.

They were sitting watching Mr. Townshend devour an enormous tea while various members of the
group took turns explaining just why his entrance
had created such a stir. While, of course, no one believed a single word the old gypsy woman had said,
they had to admit she'd been uncannily on target
concerning many areas of their lives.

"I did wonder how you knew about the waistcoat,"
Lady Harriet murmured to Colonel Melford who had
maneuvered a place beside her on the sofa. "Does he
wear the thing all the time or was it just a lucky
guess on your part?"

"I haven't the faintest notion of what you're talking about." In truth, Rawdon was more jarred by the pink waistcoat than anyone. Neither it nor Soame had played any part in his briefing.

"Don't waste your time by trying to look innocent. I've seen your fine Italian hand in all of this."

"But then you're of a naturally suspicious nature, Harry, as we all know. At least where I'm concerned."

"I'm not suspicious, just logical. And look at the choice. I can either believe that the old woman has true psychic powers or that someone filled her in on our backgrounds. And since you're the only one who could have known some of the things she told me, it therefore follows—"

"That I predicted you'd marry a handsome, red-haired stranger? Damned unlikely, I'd say."

"I didn't suggest you told her everything. She had to improvise a bit, of course."

Before he could come up with a proper answer, their conversation was interrupted by Evelyn Forbes, who was trying to organize a riding party for the next morning. "You'll come won't you, Lady Harriet? Colonel?"

Harriet begged off. She was engaged to help her hostess with ball preparations. The colonel then promptly decided to use the morning for cricket practice and said so. This plan piqued the newcomer's interest, and there was a conversational digression while he was told of the upcoming cricket match between the village and the Hall. "We're counting on you to play, Soame," his brother-in-law informed him. "Perhaps you'd like to join the colonel here and tune up your game."

"No, indeed," the other grinned. "Practice only

tends to take the edge off. I prefer to rely on the inspiration of the moment."

"What that translates to," his long-time friend explained, "is that he's a mediocre player at best, and all the practice in the world won't change that fact."

"True," Mr. Townshend amiably agreed, and everybody laughed, although his lordship and Evelyn Forbes looked slightly disappointed.

In the end, it was decided that only Selina and Susan, Evelyn and Soame would ride. Susan did her utmost to beg off, but no one would allow it. Even Selina insisted she must go. The clincher came, however, when Soame Townshend said firmly, "Come now, Miss Tunstall, don't try and toy with destiny. I'm in your stars, it seems. So the sooner we get to know each other, the better for both our sakes."

Everyone chuckled at that, a bit uncomfortably however, and Lord Fawcett soon gave the signal to retire. The party bade one another good night with far greater amiability than had previously been the case.

Mr. Townshend, though, asked his brother-in-law's permission to detain his sister for a moment, to discuss family matters, so he said. But during the coze that followed the others' departure, he managed to worm out of her just why she looked so much more drawn and far less bridelike than when he'd seen her last.

The hour had grown quite late when the brother and sister at last retired. A lump rose in Mariana's throat when she discovered that his lordship had once again elected to sleep in his dressing room. She climbed into the huge four-poster alone, trying to ward off a renewed case of the blue devils by recalling word for word the gypsy's prediction that she'd have a son. Of course, it was all just a pack of nonsense. She stretched out a hand to rest upon the empty pillow beside her. That fact was painfully obvious—pink waistcoats and other coincidences notwithstanding.

Despite what Soame Townshend had said about their entwined destinies, he did not appear eager to cultivate Miss Tunstall's acquaintance the following morning. It was, in fact, Lady Selina whom he singled out when the riding party entered a tree-lined lane that required riding two abreast.

It had been decided (by the men, both ladies had put up some resistance) that they'd ride to the gypsy camp. "I don't wish to be the only one in the house whose future catches him by surprise," Soame told Selina as they rode slowly behind the other two. "It places me at a decided disadvantage. Why, one of you could talk me into punting on a game of cards, knowing full well I was destined to lose."

"But don't you always lose, Mr. Townshend?" Her smile did little to disguise the acidity of her tongue.

Soame gave her a penetrating look. "Is that what your father told you?"

She shrugged. "I really can't recall where I gained that impression. Oh now I remember. The subject of your gambling debts came up at the dinner table. I believe that Papa settled them for you?"

"That's right," he replied evenly. "And his generosity gave you one more grudge to hold against my sister, did it not?"

"I'm sure I don't know what you mean." Selina clucked at her horse, intending to catch up with the others, but he was too quick for her. He reached over to grasp the bridle firmly. "Not so fast, Lady Selina. I'd really like to talk to you."

"I don't think we've anything to discuss, sir," she replied haughtily.

"Oh, but we do have. I'm very curious to learn just why it is you're making my sister's life miserable. Let's talk about that, shall we?"

"You, sir, are boorishly uncivil."

"Not at all. I simply believe in plain speaking. Nothing's accomplished by beating about the bush."

"I can't imagine just what you feel you've accomplished by insulting me, but if you've achieved your purpose, could we now join the others?"

"Not yet. You haven't answered my question, Lady Selina. Why have you taken so against my sister? For it's not just brotherly prejudice speaking when I say that a sweeter, more amiable female never walked the earth. Why, I'm sure she was prepared to like even you."

"*Even* me?" Lady Selina glared daggers at him. He tightened his hold on her bridle.

"That's correct. Mariana would not have been prejudiced against her husband's grown daughter. It's not in her nature, don't you see?"

"Oh yes, I can see quite plainly. I see that she's pulled the wool over the eyes of every male she's come in contact with. You're all prepared to make me the villain."

"So I'm not the first one to take you to task?" He looked pleased.

"No, indeed. In fact, you're fortunate to have found a spot in the queue that's formed."

"Care to be more specific?"

"No, why should I be? Oh very well then, what does it matter? Papa, naturally. And Evelyn."

99

"Young Forbes read you the riot act? Well now, that is interesting."

"Oh he's thoroughly smitten. Completely under your sister's spell."

"And I'll bet a monkey that he used to be one of your conquests. Well, all I can say is, you're too easily defeated. You should be able to hold your own against Mariana. You're a damned fine looking girl when you're not Friday-faced or having a fit of the sullens." His eyes traveled up and down her appreciatively.

"Is that supposed to be a compliment, Mr. Townshend? If so, you have some very odd notions of gallantry. But never mind that. I'd like you to know that I have no desire to compete with your sister."

"Of course you have. You're so jealous it's painful to see. And you're determined to ruin her and your father's marriage."

"How dare you!" she fumed. "You much mistake the matter if you think I'm jealous. Resentful, yes. Jealous, never!"

"Fustian. We won't argue the point, however. So why don't you just tell me why you 'resent' Mariana."

"Surely that's quite obvious. To you, particularly."

"Sorry, but it isn't. Suppose you enlighten me."

"I resent the fact that she deliberately set her cap to snare his fortune. Your sister married my father for his money, sir. Perhaps to some it might seem noble that she did so in part, at least, to save you from debtor's prison. But forgive me if I take a different view of the whole thing entirely."

"W-what?" Mr. Townshend stared at her in some astonishment and then began to laugh. He doubled up in the saddle and tears ran down his face.

"I fail to see what I've said that's so amusing."

"F-forgive me. It's really not all that funny, I'll grant you. But it's the idea of Mariana selling herself for twenty pounds that got to me."

"Twenty pounds!"

"That's it. Lost at faro when Fawcett and Mariana were in the metropolis on their way back here. Oh lord, what a Cheltenham tragedy you've concocted." He began to laugh again. "I hope it will comfort you to know I've brought the sum with me to repay your father. Had a glorious run of luck at White's. That's what delayed me."

"You're a habitual gambler, then." The expression on her face showed that her suspicions were once more verified.

"I do like a game of chance now and again, your ladyship. No more than most coves, though, I'll wager—if you'll forgive the expression," he chuckled, and for a minute she feared he was about to go off into spasms again. "No, you've let your imagination get the best of you, Selina. Why not admit it?"

"The fact I was mistaken about your debts has nothing to say in the matter," she shot back. "You'll surely not deny that Mariana married my father for his fortune."

"I most certainly will," he countered. "Oh, she wouldn't have married him if he was penniless, I'll grant you. My father wouldn't have permitted it. But if it was merely a fortune she was after, she had plenty of other chances. Yes, and before you say it, Fawcett wasn't the only titled gentlemen who dangled after her. The thing is, she tumbled head over heels in love with him. And I could have sworn the feeling was mutual. Till they hit the chill air of Fairoaks, that is."

Mr. Townshend observed with satisfaction that Lady Selina reddened.

Evelyn Forbes wasn't finding it quite so easy to make conversation with his partner. Miss Tunstall seemed nervous and on edge. She was oblivious to the beauty of the countryside they were riding through and replied to his polite remarks absent-mindedly.

"I say, is there something wrong?" he finally demanded.

"Wrong?" The question had at least captured her attention. "Why no, of course not. What could possibly be wrong? I'm perfectly fine, I assure you. I cannot imagine how you'd think anything could be wrong."

"Possibly because you look as if you expect to see a ghost every time we come round a bend in the lane," he answered dryly. "Or possibly because you and Selina always have your heads together as if you're plotting something. Or possibly I'm just sensitive because you ladies seem to turn up your noses at all us Berkshire yokels. I'd like to think it's nothing personal. Perhaps you just hate rusticating."

"Oh no." She turned toward him, her face quite earnest. "You do mistake the matter, Mr. Forbes. Oh, I'll admit that Selina doesn't care much for the country. She craves adventure and excitement. But I love it above all things."

"You do?" He looked at her with new interest. "Well then," he grinned, "if it ain't the country that's put you off, it must be the people."

"I'm sorry, Mr. Forbes, if I've given that impression." She did indeed look distressed. "It's just that

Selina is my dearest friend, you see, and I wouldn't wish to be disloyal."

"In other words, since she's chosen to make a perfect jackass of herself over her father's marriage, you have to go along with it."

"Oh, dear. I'd prefer you'd phrased it some other way, but I suppose that does rather sum up the situation. I must own, though," she admitted, "that Lady Fawcett is not at all what I was led to expect. But Selina does feel quite deeply about the whole thing, and well, it makes my position rather difficult," she sighed.

"Do you know what I think, Miss Tunstall?" He paused, and she shook her head. "I admire your loyalty to your friend. I do, honestly," he insisted as she looked doubtful. "All the same, I really do think you should quit letting Selina lead you."

"Oh she doesn't do that, I assure you. It's just that Selina is so ... so ... *forceful*."

"Don't I just know it," he sighed as he glanced back over his shoulder at his childhood friend. The distance between the couples had widened as the others lagged along.

Once again Miss Tunstall and Mr. Forbes lapsed into silence, but this time it was almost companionable. He kept stealing glances at her troubled face, noticing in the process that she was really quite attractive. He liked a girl with a bit of meat on her bones, unlike thin-as-a-rail Selina. Finally, "A penny for your thoughts," he said.

"I was thinking about last night, actually." She shivered a bit. "I know you'll think I'm goosish, but that old gypsy woman gave me the creeps."

"No, I don't think you're at all goosish. I didn't

much care for it myself—the way she fair looked right through a chap with those black eyes of hers, I mean. 'Creepy' is the word for it, all right."

"Do you think there's any truth to all those things she said?"

"No. Bunch of humbug," he said stoutly. "Oh, I'll admit she made my scalp crawl when some of the things she brought up were right on target. But then when I thought it over, there's a good explanation, of course."

"There is?" She brightened.

"Certainly. The old hag wouldn't have come to the Hall without being primed. And it's the easiest thing in the world to find out everything about everybody in a little place like this. Believe me, there are no secrets in Mitford."

"I do see what you mean. My village is exactly the same."

"Is it, by Jove?" He seemed to find this bit of information fascinating. "So actually there's nothing supernatural in all that mumbo jumbo. The only difference between the gypsy and all those other gossipmongers is that she stares into your palm and looks spooky while she dishes out the dirt."

Susan giggled, obviously cheered by this down-to-earth view of things.

"Of course," he added, knocking over all his newly-built defenses, "that pink waistcoat thing was a bit uncanny."

"Oh yes, it was." Her spirits sank again.

"A lucky guess, most likely. And it certainly doesn't mean you have to marry Mr. Townshend, so don't get that maggot into your head."

"No, no, of course not. It's just that the pink waistcoat thing made me wonder. I mean to say, the whole business is—unsettling. What I mean is, if the gypsy was right about that much, could she be right about other things as well? Do you think for instance, Mr. Forbes, that it would be possible for her to accurately judge the character of someone she'd never even seen?"

Cantering horses cut off his answer as they were joined by the other two.

"We thought we'd close up ranks," Mr. Townshend said. "For Lady Selina tells me the gypsy camp is just up ahead. I own that, after all I've heard, I can hardly wait to see the famous soothsayer."

"We were just talking about her," Evelyn replied. "Tell me, Townshend, you don't happen to be famous for your pink waistcoats, do you?"

"No, sorry old man. In point of fact, the one I wore last night is the only one I've ever owned. So I'm afraid you're stuck with me, Miss Tunstall." He flashed a dazzling smile her way. "The old witch really docs seem to know what she's about. I must say I can't wait to get my palm read."

He was, though, doomed to disappointment. When they arrived at the encampment, the gypsies were not there.

"Are you quite certain this was the place?"

"Sure of it." In confirmation Evelyn pointed to some scattered chicken bones and the remains of a camp fire.

"Well then I'm fated to be the only one in the group with an unread palm. But at least I'm not entirely ignorant of my future, since I was featured so prominently in someone else's fortune." He laughed then at the consternation on Miss Tunstall's face.

\* \* \*

On the way back to the Hall, they met another rider cantering up the lane. The gentleman on the high-mettled bay looked rather startled to see their party. As he nodded in passing he removed his beaver, revealing auburn hair.

"Who was that?" Mr. Townshend wondered once they were out of earshot. "He looked amazed to see us."

"Well, one doesn't expect to meet people way out here." Lady Selina tried to sound offhand. "I daresay he's looking for the gypsies, too. As to who he is, I haven't a clue. He's certainly not from around here, though."

"He's a traveler. Staying at the Magpie," Evelyn supplied. "Interested in the local scenery, so he says. Oh I say," he suddenly chuckled. "Did you happen to notice his ginger pate? You don't suppose that could be Lady Harriet's red-haired stranger, do you?"

Mr. Townshend hadn't heard that particular part of the gypsy's prediction. Lady Selina filled him in on the details while Evelyn Forbes studied Susan Tunstall, surreptitiously. For he had not missed the glance that had passed between her and the red-haired rider. Nor did he fail to notice that she'd gone pale as death.

# Chapter
# Thirteen

"WELL, WELL, WELL. Just one horse today, I see."
The colonel and his valet were coming back from
cricket practice when they spied a large bay tethered in the valley down below.

"Don't suppose they rode double, do you, sir?"
Shaftoe grinned.

At the sound of the hoofbeats, Major Mortram had
stepped out from behind the bushes, but he quickly
concealed himself again.

"No, it appears that our tall, handsome stranger
has been left waiting at the church, as it were."

"Or the young lady just hasn't had time to arrive
yet," Shaftoe observed practically.

"Come on, Jem, don't deflate me. I crossed that
gypsy's palm with silver to warn the silly peagoose
off. I'd like to think I got something for my money."

"There's no saying just how long the major's been
left dangling, a minute or an hour. But if we don't
meet Miss Tunstall on her way here," the valet concluded, "well, that's encouraging."

"And if we do meet her, I think I'll forget about
subtlety and drag the little ninnyhammer home by
the bridle."

"Let's hope she ain't coming, then. For begging your pardon in advance, sir, that would be a damn fool thing to do."

In their bedchamber at Fairoaks, the two young ladies were discussing the same issue. They faced each other across the hearth rug and were almost at daggers drawn.

"You have to go back, Susan. He'll be waiting. What's he to think?"

"What any sensible person would," Miss Tunstall retorted with more spirit than she usually displayed, "that I couldn't break away. He saw my situation."

"But he could tell we were headed home. He'll expect you to find a way to go back there and meet him."

"Then he'll soon realize it was impossible."

"But it's not impossible. All we need to say is that we're calling on a sick tenant."

"And you don't think anyone would find that odd?" Susan's tone was withering.

"Nobody but the groom is likely to know, and who cares what he thinks. Come on, let's hurry."

"No. This is absurd. Major Mortram would never have waited so long."

Lady Selina stared at her friend in amazement. Her eyes widened with a sudden revelation. "You don't want to go, do you, Susan?"

"Isn't that just what I've been saying?"

"You know perfectly well what I mean. Even if we hadn't been practically forced to go out riding with those two, I bet a monkey you still would have cried off. You're scared. Admit it!"

"I am not scared." Susan walked over and sat down

on the window seat. "I just don't like being rushed into things, that's all."

"Yes, you are afraid." Selina followed and stood over her accusingly. "In point of fact, you've been acting most strange ever since you had your fortune told. Just what did that old hag say to you to put you into such a taking?"

"I told you."

Her friend studied Susan through narrowed eyes. "I don't believe you've told me everything. No, by heaven, that gypsy must have said something about the major or you wouldn't be behaving so oddly. So out with it, Susan. What did she tell you?"

Bit by bit, Selina wormed out the story of the gypsy's warning. "Surely you don't believe such nonsense," she said scornfully.

"I don't know what to believe anymore." Tears gathered in Susan's eyes. "She was right about other things. Admit it."

"That confounded pink waistcoat! That's what's upset you. Chances are it was merely a lucky guess. Or even more likely," she added thoughtfully, "one of the gypsy band saw Mr. Townshend on his way here and tipped her off."

"Would there have been time?" Susan objected. "She was here ages before Mr. Townshend came."

"Well, then, perhaps Soame Townshend stopped in at the Magpie for a while and one of the gypsies just happened to be there. That would have given loads of time to get the word back to the old crone."

"Fustian."

"Well, you can't expect me to know exactly how it was done," Selina snapped. "But you can be sure of one thing. It was a trick."

Though Miss Tunstall clamped her lips tight shut, she still looked unconvinced.

"Very well then. If you prefer to believe you're doomed to marry Soame Townshend—a self-confessed fortune hunter, by the by—rather than the man who truly loves you, well, I wash my hands of you, Susan. There's no hope."

"Of course I don't think I'm doomed to marry Mr. Townshend."

"All right then, there you are. And you do love Major Mortram, don't you?"

"Y-yes. It's just that . . ."

"Just what, Susan?" Selina prodded as her friend's voice trailed off.

"An elopement! I just cannot like the idea of an elopement. It seems so—so—rackety."

"Well, I think it's the most romantic thing in the world. I'd certainly do it in a minute."

"I know you would," the other sighed.

"Besides, what choice do you have?" Lady Selina asked practically. "Your mother will never give her consent, and you know perfectly well your guardian won't go against her wishes."

"I do know. And what's more, I think Sir Rawdon suspects something. He keeps looking at me—oddly."

"Of course he looks at you oddly. Who could blame him after the way you dropped your breakfast plate and screeched at the sight of him. He probably expects you're a candidate for Bedlam." She was momentarily diverted. "It's a pity, you know, that we have to shun him. I really rather wish he weren't the enemy, for he's certainly handsome, is he not? Lady Harriet was a fool, to my way of thinking. But then, of course, he's not as divinely handsome as your major." She returned to the subject at hand. "Oh Susan, the way that man looks at you! Why, it makes me almost melt. I can't imagine the effect it must have on you."

"Then you do believe he loves me?"

"Of course he loves you. To follow you here to this godforsaken place. Why, it's too romantic for words. I only wish it were happening to me."

Her friend was almost of the same opinion.

Selina was quick to pick up on this ambivalence, and, as usual, made up Susan's mind. "You're right. It is too late now to think of meeting the major today. Here's what you must do. Write him a note explaining just what happened and arrange another rendezvous. There's still plenty of time to work out the details of your elopement. And don't worry so, Susan, dear. I'll help you with everything. And it will all be for the best, you'll see. For once you're married, and your mother really gets to know Major Mortram, she'll come around. For who could resist those soulful eyes?" Selina jumped up from the window seat and hurried to the writing desk. Before her friend could have second thoughts, she pulled out a sheet of paper and a freshly sharpened quill. "Now here you are, my dear. Everything's ready. Come on, Susan, write!"

# Chapter
# Fourteen

Down in the servants' hall, Jem Shaftoe was more than happy to come to the aid of the footman who'd been ordered to carry Miss Tunstall's letter. That disgruntled young man had had plans to sneak away and meet the girl he was walking out with. She lived in the opposite direction from the Magpie.

"Be glad to deliver the note," the valet offered. "Just so happens I'm on me way to the Magpie now."

"There'll most likely be an answer."

"Then I'll wait for it."

"Wot I mean to say is, the young ladies will expect me to be the one to bring it back, since I'm sworn to secrecy and all." He gave a roguish grin that included the other sharers of the "secret," the entire household staff now gathered round the large oaken table at their dinner.

"Well, two hours should give you time enough to cuddle your sweetheart a bit and still get back in time to take the answer up."

"But wot if the major 'appens to mention you, and then Miss Tunstall realizes as how it wasn't me who brought him her letter? I've always done it before, don't you see."

112

"Now do you seriously think they're going to be discussing servants? And frankly, I doubt if the major—if that's what he is—ever really looked at you. Still, don't let me talk you into anything. Take it yourself, if you'd rather."

The footman required no further persuasion, and a little later Jem Shaftoe was striding into the Magpie with Miss Tunstall's letter in his pocket.

A quick look around the crowded taproom satisfied him that Major Mortram was not among the company. Neither was Rosina Flack behind the bar. Shaftoe hoped that these two circumstances were just coincidental.

"Looking for someone?" an arch voice inquired from the hallway directly behind him.

He focused all his willpower upon turning around quite casually. Once he'd accomplished that difficult feat, he was once more in danger of being overset by the fact that Miss Flack was looking unusually fetching in a sprigged muslin frock, cut considerably lower in the bosom area than decorum called for. Shaftoe blocked his mind against a vision of her leaning across the bar. "As a matter of fact, I was," he assured her evenly. "Have you seen Major Mortram around?"

"And just what makes you think I keep tabs on Major Mortram?"

"Well now, I didn't mean to put you in a taking. What's the matter, love? Did you really think I'd come here to look for you?"

She put a hand on her hip and tried to look disdainful. "I really didn't give it any thought at all. But if I had done, I'd have known you were fetching and carrying for the gentry."

"You could say so, I suppose. Though to be more

113

accurate, I'm fetching and carrying for Jack the footman. So tell me, love, is the major in his room?"

"I'm not your love, but as far as I know, he is."

"And just where might that be?"

"Go up the stairs, turn left, second door on your left."

"Now wait a minute, love. You lost me. What I mean to say is, I'll never find it by myself."

"None too bright then, are you?"

"Best you take me there. You wouldn't want me wandering your halls, sticking me nose in the wrong rooms—yours, for instance—now would you?" He gave her a engaging grin.

"You're hopeless, that's what you are all right."

But for all her withering tone, she seemed willing enough to guide him. Shaftoe followed her up the steps, his eyes appreciative of her neat figure and trim ankles.

They'd only made it around the corner she'd described when he reached out a hand to stop her. "I'm really not in such a tearing hurry," he breathed as he pulled her into his arms.

"You do seem to think you can make a habit of this sort of thing, now don't you?" In spite of the protest, Shaftoe noted that the struggle she was putting up was not wholehearted. "I must say, you London coves are fast workers."

"I'm not a London cove," he murmured, looking at her luscious lips. "But I plead guilty to the other charge. I've got to work fast, love. It ain't often I can catch you between beaux." He kissed her then, taking no small satisfaction from the fact that he had to bend a bit to do it. And he found the experience immensely pleasurable. Even more so than on the first occasion, since this time Miss Flack seemed resigned to her fate and cooperated most pleasantly.

"I think you'd best go the rest of the way yourself." She frowned severely when they finally broke for air.

"Go? Go where?" He shook his head to clear it.

"Why to find the major, simpleton." She gave him an arch look, a shove in the right direction, and then went flouncing back toward the stairs.

In spite of his stated fears, Shaftoe had remarkably little trouble locating the major's room. He stood respectfully by and surveyed the small, but well-appointed, chamber while Mortram read his message. The contents didn't seem to please the gentleman over much, for he frowned and reread it more than once. Then he stared unseeingly at the high four-poster that took up most of the room's floor space.

After shifting a bit from foot to foot, Shaftoe coughed politely. "Will there be an answer, sir?" He'd been hoping for a quick pint downstairs before he was due back at the Hall.

"What's that?" The major snapped out of his reverie. "Oh yes, there'll be an answer." He seated himself at a small rosewood table and assembled his writing materials. He even went so far as to dip his pen into the ink. Composition did not appear to come easily, however. After a false start or two he glanced back over his shoulder at the valet and remarked, a bit too casually, "I understand there's a new visitor at the Hall."

"Why yes, sir. That would be Mr. Townshend, her ladyship's brother."

"Dangling after Miss Tunstall then, is he?"

The fact that the major had turned his face away and was diligently wiping his quill did not disguise the importance of the question. Shaftoe studied the back of the well-shaped head while an idea germinated.

"Why no, I wouldn't say so, sir." He appeared to be mulling the question over. "Oh, Mr. Townshend has quite a way with all the ladies, sir. I'd say he flirts a bit with everyone in skirts more or less by instinct. But no," he concluded firmly, "there's no way he could possibly be seriously interested in Miss Tunstall."

"And why ever not?" The major looked slightly insulted as he shifted his chair around to continue the conversation.

"Oh, nothing at all against the young lady, sir," the valet said hastily. "It's just that—" He shifted his feet and looked uncomfortable. "I really shouldn't be saying this out loud, you understand, sir, but it's generally known that Mr. Townshend's pockets are to let, and that he's dangling after a fortune."

"Well, there you are then. Miss Tunstall's an heiress, so I've heard."

"Well, yes and no."

He now had the major's full attention. "Yes and no? What the devil's that supposed to mean?"

"Why, just that while it is true that Miss Tunstall will *eventually* come into a tidy fortune, it won't happen till she's twenty-five."

"Twenty-five!" The major suddenly choked. "Are you certain of that?" He looked at Shaftoe suspiciously.

"Oh yes, sir. Dead certain. You see I happen to be in the employ of Colonel Melford, the young lady's guardian. And I've heard him mention the matter more than once. So you see, sir, that would rule her out where Mr. Townshend's concerned. He's the impatient type, don't you see, and would want a much quicker return than that on his invested time. No indeed, sir. He's not dangling after Miss Tunstall. It's Lady Harriet Fane he's interested in."

"But I was given to understand that Lady Harriet is practically a pauper. Lives on her scribbling—or so I've been told."

"Oh that was true, sir," the valet concurred. "But the fact is, she's due to come into a fortune anytime."

"Oh for God's sake!" The major laughed derisively. "The gypsy. It's been the talk of the barroom, all the preposterous things she told 'em at the Hall. Why, the gardener expects to dig up buried treasure."

"Does he now?" Shaftoe, a country boy himself, could still be amazed at the speed with which news traveled in that environment. "Well now, I couldn't say, sir, about the gardener's chances. But in the case of Lady Harriet, it so happens that the old gypsy hit the nail square on the head. For Lady Harriet's uncle in the north is dying."

"Oh?" The major's eyebrows conveyed his skepticism. "Odd that no one around here has mentioned her prospects. I take it you're implying the uncle's rich."

"Regular nabob, sir. And the fact that he's not mentioned ain't really all that odd." He lowered his voice and looked disapproving. "Trade."

"Trade?"

"That's correct, sir. You might say it's been the skeleton in the Fane closet," he improvised, "that the late Lady Fane's brother owns several mills somewhere in the north. And a deuced good thing for Lady Harriet it is, sir, for she's his sole living relative. And the fact is, he's hovering."

"Hovering?"

There was a moment of silence while Shaftoe allowed this taradiddle to sink in. "And so you can see, sir, that Miss Tunstall has nothing to fear from Mr. Townshend. For like I said, he's the impatient sort. A bird in the hand, if you'll excuse the comparison, would always be more attractive to Mr. Townshend than an eight-year wait to catch a better one in the bush."

"Yes, I can see that." The major was looking very thoughtful.

"Then, too," Shaftoe pressed his point, "there's also the fact that Lady Harriet's much easier pickings."

"Oh? How so?"

"A bit long in the tooth, don't you know. Oh, she's overripe for marriage, no mistake. Not like some seventeen-year-old schoolroom miss with visions of suitors yet to come. Lady Harriet's growing desperate, don't you see?"

"Why yes, I collect that would be the case." The major stared off into space for a bit longer, then seemed to get his scattered wits together. At any rate, he turned back to his paper and dashed off a communiqué with record speed. He applied a bit of sealing wax, then handed Shaftoe the folded paper. The valet hesitated just a bit, but when it became apparent that no coin was to be forthcoming, he ducked his head toward the major and left the room. As he closed the door behind him, a broad grin split his face.

His jubilant mood evaporated, however, when he entered the barroom and saw Rosina Flack seated on a bench next to her farmer. Shaftoe decided to forgo his pint, after all.

118

# Chapter
# Fifteen

COLONEL RAWDON MELFORD lowered the book he was reading, and a pleased smile lit up his face. Lady Harriet Fane was entering the library. The smile wavered a bit as he noted the storminess of her expression.

"I've been looking all over for you, Rawdon," she snapped.

"Oh? Want someone to ride with you this morning, do you?" His appreciative eyes took in her neat, gray habit with its tall cork hat set at an angle on her fiery hair. As he'd remarked before, Harriet was at her best in riding costume. Also, a flushed face and snapping eyes became her, he decided, which was fortune since he so often put her in a temper.

"No, I am not looking for someone to ride with." She crossed the room to loom over him as he sat sprawled in a leather wing-back chair, his feet resting on a matching footstool. "I've already had my ride. To my cottage, I might add. And now I'm here to tell you that if you don't keep that mongrel of yours shut up, I'll—I'll—shoot it!"

"No you won't, Harry," he replied calmly. "You couldn't possibly. It ain't in you to hurt an animal."

"All right then," she stormed, "I'll shoot *you*!"

"Now that sounds more reasonable. Could you possibly simmer down and tell me what's caused you to fly off into the boughs? What's poor old Adolphus done now?"

"You know perfectly well what he's done!"

"Has he, by Jove?" A grin lit up the colonel's face. "Why, the old dog!"

"It's not funny, Rawdon. My Christobel's a thoroughbred. There's no better strain around. I'd planned to breed her, dammit, and sell the litter at a premium price."

"Did you, Harry?" He looked concerned. "Well then, tell you what I'll do. I'll buy the pups myself. Every last one of the little mongrels at the going rate for aristocratic greyhounds."

"I don't want your charity."

"Oh it won't be charity, I assure you. Those dogs will be a source of constant satisfaction. Every time I look at them I'll think of true love surmounting all barriers of class and creed."

"Fustian. Love has nothing to say in the matter. That oversexed mutt just jumped the fence, that's all."

"Enterprising, ain't he?" The grin broadened.

"Comes from long association with you, I collect."

"I'm not sure if I'm being insulted or complimented."

"Oh, are you not? Well, I'll be glad to clear the matter up then."

"Never mind. But to get back to the issue at hand, I really see no reason for you to turn this business into a Cheltenham tragedy. Christobel won't care whether or not her whelps are blue bloods."

"The silly bitch has no taste whatever."

"Now there's where you're wrong. Your problem, Harry, is that you, like most folk, judge by superficialities. Underneath his motley, Adolphus is a regular prince.

"But as I was saying, your bitch won't mind that her litter doesn't come up to snuff, and I'll buy the pups and everything will be right and tight then."

"Well," she sounded a bit appeased, "I don't know that it will actually come down to that. I don't think your Adolphus impregnated her."

He looked aghast. "Don't tell me the old fellow couldn't do it. By George, now I am shocked."

"Oh he could do it, all right. The thing is, I doused them with a pail of water and separated them. I trust in time."

"You didn't!"

"Of course I did. You don't think I'd stand idly by and let that happen if I could prevent it."

"No, of course not. Well, well. The old water treatment again. By gad, Harry, you seem to think that's the answer for everything."

"Must you constantly fling that episode in my face?" she blazed. "Still though, as I've pointed out, I suppose there is some parallel between your dog and you. You're both threats to the female population."

"You give me too much credit," he said modestly, "but Adolphus thanks you."

"Let's not wander off the subject. What I came here to say is this—you keep that mutt away from my greyhound."

"And just how am I supposed to accomplish that?"

"That's your problem. Pen him up, I suppose."

"That's cruel, Harry. Dolph's a true free spirit."

"That's the point, you ninnyhammer. I don't want him making free with my Christobel."

"Then pen *her* up. Oh that's right, I forgot. You said you did. High fence, was it?"

"Yes, but not high enough, obviously."

"Well, there you are then. Just proves my point: love knows no barriers. You really shouldn't be so hard-hearted, Harry."

"Don't call me Harry." She sighed then at the futility of trying to have a sensible conversation with him. "And pray do something about that animal of yours." She turned to leave, but he reached out a hand to detain her.

"Why is it, Harry, that you always have to turn tail and run every time we're alone together?"

"I'm not 'turning tail.' I said what I've come to say, and there's an end to it."

"Sit down a minute, won't you? I really do need to talk to you on a most important matter. And no need to look like that. It's not about us. Sit down a minute, will you?"

She hesitated, then shrugged and took a seat. "I can spare a *minute,* I suppose."

"Do you have to be so damn literal? You surely don't plan to time me."

"Say whatever it is you wish to say, Rawdon."

"Gad, you're hostile. Would it help if I cleared the air and apologized for barging into your bedchamber the other night?"

"It would not. Though I confess I'm astonished you even recall it, given your condition."

"Of course I recall it. Most pleasantly, I might add. In fact, I recall all the times I made love to you. The apple orchard, in particular, springs to mind."

She colored a bit, then stared at him frostily. "I'm amazed that among all your 'romantic' interludes, you'd remember such a trivial episode."

"Nothing trivial about it, dammit."

"Well I'd forgotten it until this very minute when you brought it up."

"Had you, Harry?" His steady gaze appeared to bore right through her.

"Yes." She met the challenge. "I made a point of forgetting. My gullibility is not a thing I'm proud of. You were down from Oxford—and God knows how many conquests you'd had by then. You took advantage of my naïveté."

"Now just one blasted minute! I did not take advantage. There's no way I'd forget a thing like that. It wasn't easy, mind you, but I always played the gentleman with you. Confound it, woman, I planned to marry you."

"I wasn't implying that you rolled me in the hay," she said dryly.

What he had done was, in her opinion, far, far worse. He'd made her fall in love with him. "But your minute's more than up." She rose to her feet. "And you've kept me here under false pretenses. You did say we weren't going to talk about us."

"Don't be so dashed prickly." He stood to take her firmly by the shoulders and push her back down into her chair. "Very well, then, the discussion of the stormy, but memorable—to one of us, at least—relationship of Lady Harriet and Sir Rawdon is at an end. It's the Flacks I really wished to ask you about."

"The innkeeper and his daughter? What about them?"

"Know 'em well, do you?"

"Fairly well, I'd say. Surely you recall what village life is like."

"You mean the place we grew up in wasn't unique? I could have sworn there was no other spot on earth where everyone could know everyone else's business that completely. I still believe our gossipmongers have no peers."

"Sorry to disillusion you. Mitford's no different. So what do you wish to know about the Flacks?"

"Well, first of all, is she good enough for Shaftoe?"

"The fair Rosina? Hmmm. That is a poser. Well, you've seen her, of course."

"She's a real head turner. No doubt on that score. But that's not what I asked."

"Well, I question whether you'll think any woman is good enough for Jem Shaftoe. But given the fact that he seems to be in love with her, well, let's just say that if she happened to feel the same, yes, I expect she could fill the bill. She's a shameless flirt, of course. And flighty in one sense. But in another, she's down-to-earth practical. She's been her father's right hand for years. I imagine she knows about as much about running the Magpie as he does. Yes," Harriet mused, "I can't say I've ever given the matter much thought, but I suspect that underneath all her sauciness, little Miss Flack does have a brain."

"I collect you would notice a thing like that."

"And I collect that with Rosina's other—advantages—you wouldn't."

"Touché. Now what about her father? Why has he taken against Shaftoe?"

"It's natural enough if you stop and think about it. Oh nothing personal, so don't get your hackles up. It's just that Rosina's an only child, and he's ambitious for her. You really can't blame the man. Joel Holton's a good catch. Owns a nice property."

"Hmmm. So if Shaftoe had better prospects, he'd be in the running?"

"Well, I expect if Rosina wanted him he could be. I don't think, all things being equal or nearly so, that Mr. Flack would like to lock horns with Rosina. She's used to her own way, you know."

"Name me a female who isn't," he muttered.

"If that answers your question, I'll go now." Once again, though, he put out a hand to detain her.

"No, just one more thing." He lowered his voice in case the walls had ears. "What do you make of our host and hostess?"

"What do you mean, what do I make of them?"

"Oh come on. You know them better than I do. You're well acquainted with Fawcett, at any rate. By the by, did he ever come courting you?"

"No."

"Well that lowers my opinion of him a bit. But back to the subject at hand. You aren't going to tell me you haven't noticed that things seem to be at sixes and sevens with them."

"No, I'm not going to tell you that, for I don't think we should be having this discussion."

"They're not sleeping together, you know."

Her eyes widened. "I *don't* know. I *shouldn't* know. And just how you—oh. Shaftoe, of course."

"You don't think a thing like that wouldn't be chewed over in the servants' hall, now do you?"

"I collect not. But we're supposed to be their betters. So I suggest we drop the subject."

"Rather than flying off into the high boughs, I think it would be more to the point if you tried to help."

125

"I am trying. I've been working with Mariana on the ball arrangements and trying to teach her a bit about running a place this size. She's quite intimidated, you know."

"Hang the housekeeping! I'm talking about the marriage. My God, woman, they should still be on their honeymoon, and they're in separate beds!"

"Well, you surely can't think there's anything I can do about that."

"I thought we might talk to them."

She stared in disbelief. "You're bamming me."

"No, I'm serious. Oh, I don't mean together. I'll talk to Fawcett, and you could have a word with Mariana."

She choked suddenly, and then went off into peals of laughter.

"I don't see what's so hilarious," he said huffily, once she'd subsided a bit. "I think the matter's serious."

"I know it is," she agreed as she wiped her streaming eyes. "But the notion of us—you and me—giving marital advice—it's—too—too." She went off into another laughing fit, then finally managed to say, "The idea's too ridiculous for words."

"Well, I'm not so sure," he answered seriously. "Oh, in the normal way of things I'd certainly agree. But this ain't normal. It may have escaped your notice, Harry, but we're getting along better than just about anyone on the premises. Our host and hostess are in separate beds. Lady Selina's not just at daggers drawn with her papa and stepmama, she's feuding with young Forbes and Soame Townshend, too. And whatever attitude she happens to strike goes for my feather-brained godchild as well. By the by, I must say I'm a little disappointed in Soame. I rather expected him to pour oil on the troubled waters. He's an amiable soul as a rule, but he certainly seems to have taken against young Selina."

"Oh do you think so?" She looked amused.

"Know it for a fact. Told me he gave her a regular tongue banging for the way she's been treating his sister."

"Well, good for him."

"Oh, I agree he was justified, but it didn't add much to the jolliness of our gathering. You do see my point, Harry. You and I are the only noncombatants in the group. So I think it really is up to us to help straighten out this mess."

"No, it isn't." Her tone was decisive as she stood up once more. "You've overlooked one important thing, Colonel Melford. Where you and I are concerned, there is no 'us.' And I have things to do, even if you have not. So I'll bid you good day now."

After she'd closed the library door with more emphasis than he really thought was necessary, Rawdon picked up the book he'd been struggling to read. He'd chosen it for the sole reason that he knew it was a favorite of Harriet's. "Damned silly story," he glared at it. "No wonder it appeals to females. The title's the only thing that makes the slightest sense. It is well named, I'll give it that. *Pride and Prejudice*. Harry's both 'em."

He flung the offending volume across the room.

# Chapter
# Sixteen

"Could someone explain to me," the colonel inquired the next morning when everyone, for once, had met together in the breakfast parlor, "just why the village of Mitford holds its Maying in July?"

"You know, I've never really thought about it." Evelyn Forbes's forkful of ham paused en route to his mouth. "We just always have done so." He devoured the morsel.

"We're practical folk in these parts," Lord Fawcett smiled. "May's treacherous. But early July—the days are longest, the weather's finest, flowers and leaves are plentiful. Everybody's ready to be outdoors."

"Besides, what's in a name?" Harriet asked.

"Quite a bit, I'd say," was Soame Townshend's opinion. "Whoever heard of a Julypole? Or going Julying?"

Everyone laughed, and Lady Selina joined the conversation, displaying the most enthusiasm she'd exhibited since her father's wedding. "It really is loads of fun. Everybody comes. The entire village. And all our friends. Everyone gives their servants the day off. All the farmers let their fields go. There'll be games—and exhibits—all kinds of food." She turned shyly toward her stepmama. "You'll like it above all things, Mariana."

That lady managed to mask her astonishment with a smile. "I'm sure I shall. I'm looking forward to it," she said.

Lord Fawcett eyed his daughter with approval. Both Mr. Forbes and Mr. Townshend were looking rather smug.

It was decided that the young ladies, accompanied by Evelyn and Soame, would go to the common that morning to observe the preparations and volunteer their services wherever appropriate. "And we'll take the flowers," Selina said. "The gardener should have them ready."

"I hope they were careful to save enough blossoms for our ball," Mariana worried. "Thank goodness the roses are at their peak."

"They'd best keep a sharp lookout at that." His lordship chuckled. "It wouldn't be the first time that the village children slipped into our garden and stripped it bare for the Maying. I spoke to William Flack about it the other day. He promised me he'd put a flea in their ears."

"What's William Flack got to do with it?" Rawdon asked.

"Oh, he's in charge of our Maying," Evelyn told him.

"A born organizer if there ever was one," Lord Fawcett added.

"Well, it all sounds quite interesting."

"Come to the green with us, Rawdon," Soame invited with more civility than pressure.

"Can't this morning. I'm going to practice bowling a bit more."

"You're really taking this match seriously, aren't you?"

"Certainly. The honor of the Hall and all that sort of thing."

"Well, as long as you don't expect the rest of us to share your zeal."

"Believe me, Soame, I expect nothing. I've seen you play. You children run along and build your Maypole or whatever. I expect I'll see you in the afternoon."

The colonel then excused himself and went to collect his valet. The Ladies Fawcett and Fane planned to spend the day in final preparations for the ball, which was to be held on the evening following the Maying. Lord Fawcett went off to closet himself with his bailiff, who, like everyone else, would be on holiday the following day.

The young ladies hurried to their bedchamber to dress for the outing. "You have to make up your mind, Susan," Selina urged as she tied the blue satin ribbons of a becoming chip-straw bonnet underneath her chin. Both girls were wearing their most stylish walking dresses, but for once, they were quite unconscious of the picture that they made.

"I don't see why I have to decide anything today," Susan protested. "You read Brent's note. He refused to put any pressure on me. He told me to take all the time I wished."

"Yes, but he's only being chivalrous. I've explained that if you're going to elope, the night of the ball's perfect. Indeed it's probably the only opportunity you'll get. It's the only time they'll not be watching us like hawks."

"You make us sound like prisoners or something. And really everyone's been most kind."

"I wasn't being literal, Susan. But with so few of us in the house, *anyone's* absence becomes noticeable. But the night of the ball's perfect. In all that crush, why you could be gone for hours with no one the wiser."

"Oh Selina, I just don't know."

"Really, Susan, you are chickenhearted."

"But an elopement's so—so—"

"Romantic?"

"I was going to say 'shocking.' "

"But what choice have you? You surely aren't prepared to give Major Mortram up?"

"N-no."

"So there you are, then. Oh really, Susan, you worry too much." She gave her friend an impulsive squeeze and then a little shake. "Oh, I'd give anything to be in your shoes, with the divine major ready to carry me off. Well then, it's settled?" Miss Tunstall nodded. "Capital! I'll manage to see Major Mortram today, then, and make the final arrangements with him. Come on." She tugged her friend by the hand. "We'd best be going. You know how gentlemen hate being made to wait."

Since the day was fine, the foursome elected to walk to the common. Each carrying a basket piled high with flowers, they set out in high good humor, with the exception, that is, of Miss Tunstall, who was definitely having second thoughts. Lady Selina and Mr. Townshend, talking a mile a minute, soon outstripped the other two. Evelyn, the native, seemed to think it incumbent upon him to prepare his less-than-enthusiastic companion for the treats in store. When he described, hilariously, a donkey race he'd participated in the year before, he was gratified to see her slough off her fit of the blue devils and giggle appreciatively. Encouraged, he began another anecdote, while she thought how comfortable to be with he was.

The common was a lovely greensward of approximately twenty acres, surrounded by fields, farmhouses, cottages and wooded uplands. When the party from the Hall arrived, the place was abuzz with people and activity. The landlord of the Magpie was everywhere at once, overseeing every aspect of the various preparations necessary to insure a successful Maying. He swooped down on the proffered flower baskets enthusiastically and put the foursome to work weaving garlands for the May House, while tactfully rejecting Mr. Forbes's offer that he and Mr. Townshend join the work party that was constructing booths.

As they settled underneath a spreading tree to begin the work of garland making, Evelyn sounded a bit affronted. "He acts as if we'd just be in the way out there."

"Well I, for one, would be," Soame retorted. "I thought you'd lost your mind when you offered. Shade and fair company. That's my idea of a perfect day. Well, almost perfect," he amended. "Tell me, why was it we didn't fill one of these baskets with food and a bottle of wine instead of all these flowers? Pathetic lack of foresight, I'd call it."

Selina and Evelyn hastened to reassure him that some of the booths being set up for the morrow would be enterprising enough to begin selling their wares to the bevy of workers and onlookers today. "In a way, this is as much a part of the Maying as tomorrow is," Selina explained.

"That's all very well for some, but after I paid off my debt to your father, I'm sorry to report that my pockets are to let. That's why it's such a relief to know I've an heiress in my future." He leered at Susan who turned pink.

"Look here." Mr. Forbes frowned, "I don't think you should keep harping on that stupid gypsy business. You're embarrassing Miss Tunstall."

"Then I beg Miss Tunstall's pardon. I certainly did not wish to do so."

"We don't need money," Selina hastily interposed. "Papa will settle with Mr. Flack."

"That won't be necessary," Evelyn told her.

"Well breeched then, are you?" Mr. Townshend sounded genuinely interested. "Oops, sorry," he added as Evelyn shot him a repressive look. "Not good ton to inquire, I collect."

This temporary awkwardness quickly evaporated, however, as the foursome succumbed to the festive mood around them. They were soon remarking on the variety of people who swarmed about the place. The bevy of children running and squealing in everybody's way were especially delightful.

Evelyn laughed as someone plucked off a five-year-old urchin who was determined to climb the Maypole while it was being raised. "Remember when we were that age and used to come here, Selina?"

"Oh yes," she smiled back at him.

"You know, this really doesn't seem so very different from a folk festival I attended once in Portugal," Soame remarked.

"Why, when were you ever in Portugal?" Susan asked.

"During that little altercation we had with Bonaparte."

"You served abroad?" Selina blurted. "I didn't know that. I thought you were—"

"A Bond Street beau? Pink of the ton? Rake and gambler?" Soame supplied. "All that came later, after I'd sold out."

"I had no idea."

"Of course you hadn't. But if you'd been on speaking terms with my sister, I'm certain she would have been delighted to fill you in. I'm one of her favorite subjects, actually."

"It must have been a splendid adventure."

"The war? Well, an adventure certainly. I'm not sure the term 'splendid' quite applies."

"Oh, I didn't mean that part, actually being in battle," Selina shuddered. "That would be dreadful. No, what I meant was the travel. Seeing new places and people with different languages and different ways of living. That's the sort of thing I was referring to."

"I couldn't agree more heartily. In fact, I'm hoping to get into the foreign service and go live abroad. That's why I stayed so long in London—well, that and other things. I had to talk with some government coves. And I don't mind admitting that I kept dragging the name of my brother-in-law, Lord Fawcett, into the interview quite shamelessly."

"Oh, I do envy you so. I wish I were a man."

"That would be a pity." Soame smiled into the earnest, gray eyes under the chip-straw bonnet. "You being a man, I mean. A decided waste of good material."

134

"Well, I certainly wouldn't wish to live anywhere but England," Evelyn declared when he'd finished sucking the blood from a thorn prick in his thumb. "Can't see why anyone would, when it comes to that."

"I know one thing. I'd never understand a word of another language," Susan sighed.

"That's true," Selina agreed. "You were the despair of Mademoiselle Beauvoir who tried to teach you French."

"Don't remind me," her friend shuddered. "I was never so happy as when I left school."

"And how did you do in French, Lady Selina?" Mr. Townshend looked genuinely interested.

"Oh, she took to it like a native, or so Mademoiselle Beauvoir said," Susan supplied, while Lady Selina looked appropriately embarrassed.

"Complete waste of time if you ask me," Evelyn Forbes declared.

The morning was speeding by quickly. The foursome had a good view of the Magpie's booth-in-progress and began laying wagers as to how soon it would be in operation. "I say, I've seen that fellow somewhere before," Soame remarked when a tall, handsome gentleman in a bottle-green coat and yellow pantaloons joined the line that began to form in front of the booth.

"You've seen him everywhere is more likely," Evelyn said. "When we were coming back from the gypsy camp, for one. Nobody's sure just what he's up to or why he keeps hanging around here. He says he's just a tourist."

"Well he can't be a French spy, that's for sure. The war's over."

The object under discussion must have felt their

eyes upon him, for at that moment he turned in their direction. Even at a distance, it was plain to see that he looked startled.

"That's odd," Soame remarked. "Was he looking at us?"

As if in answer to that question, Miss Rosina Flack came sauntering by. She was dressed in a fetching white muslin gown with a red ribbon sash run just below her enticing bosom. The brim of the straw hat perched atop her raven curls was weighted down with genuine blood red roses.

"Well that explains that," Soame murmured. "There's something to make any man's eyes bug out."

Evelyn didn't answer. He was studying Susan Tunstall's stricken face. It occurred to him that she'd changed quite a bit in the short time he'd known her. For one thing, she appeared to be growing thinner. For another, she seemed weighted down with care.

The gentlemen gathered up the completed garlands to be delivered before they joined the thinning ranks of customers in front of the temporary Magpie. No sooner had they left than Selina nudged her friend. "Now's your chance." Major Mortram was standing a bit aloof from a group of people, watching the final touches being put on the May House. Mr. Forbes and Mr. Townshend had given the stranger appraising glances as they passed by, but now their backs were turned his way while they waited for their food to be prepared.

"What do you mean, 'my chance'? My chance for what?" Susan looked positively panicked.

"To speak to Major Mortram, goose, and tell him what's been decided. Hurry. There's no time to lose."

"I can't just walk up to him in front of everyone. What will people think?"

"They won't realize you're talking to him if you do it right. You just stand close by, but not actually looking at him, don't you see, and whisper out of the corner of your— Oh for heaven's sake, Susan, Evelyn and Soame will be back before I can explain everything to you. Never mind." She jumped to her feet and smoothed out her skirt. "I'll go. It will be simpler in the long run."

"Oh Selina, I don't really think—" But Susan's protest fell on empty space. Her friend was hurrying across the grassy common.

"Where's Selina got to?" Evelyn asked as the gentlemen returned with a basket heavily laden with chicken, ham, fruit, and tart to be washed down with claret.

"She wanted a closer look at the May House," Susan improvised, and they all stared in that direction. Selina was standing to the right and slightly behind the red-haired gentleman who seemed completely enthralled, as was she, by the construction of a wall of bright green leaves, and never took his eyes off of it. Try though she might, Susan was unable to detect any movement of her friend's lips. Evelyn, however, was more discerning. He remembered the spy games they'd played as children.

A little later, as the foursome consumed their alfresco meal, Selina managed to whisper in her friend's ear, "Everything's settled."

"Oh," was the laconic answer.

# Chapter
# Seventeen

JEM SHAFTOE STOOD at the edge of the greensward and surveyed the bustling panorama. His eyes swept over the picnickers from the Hall. They noted Major Mortram, who seemed to have lost his fascination with the May House, and was strolling back toward the makeshift Magpie. Next they located Landlord Flack, who was trying to arbitrate a spirited squabble over one piece of turf that had been claimed as a site for two rival booths. Shaftoe's eyes then moved on till they sighted their true target, Miss Rosina Flack. This young lady had been abandoned by a father who was in thrall to a higher calling, Master of the May Day Revels. She was frantically trying to serve the hoard of clamoring patrons alone.

Shaftoe strolled over to the booth and stepped behind the counter. "Here, let me help you, love," he offered.

"And just how do you expect to manage that? It's food and drink they're wanting, Mr. Shaftoe, not to have their coats brushed and their cravats tied."

"Just you watch me," Jem replied, tying on the landlord's voluminous apron. He hoisted another keg up on the rude planks that did service as a bar and began to tap it. They worked swiftly, without a word between them. Miss Flack, however, stole several glances at her partner. She was gaining a grudging respect for his efficiency, until he spilled a quantity of dark, foaming beer on Major Mortram's bottle-green coat sleeve.

"Clumsy!" she whispered as the major swore.

"Deft's more like it," he answered with a grin as he began to wipe the counter.

William Flack was well aware of what was going on. The problem was, he couldn't extricate himself from his duties as Master of the Revels to do anything about it. Jem Shaftoe had been behind the bar nearly an hour before the publican was finally free to go boot him out.

Flack was hurrying toward his booth when he found his way blocked by a tall, distinguished gentleman, sporting glorious, dark side whiskers and a luxurious mustache. "Good day to you, Colonel." Mr. Flack tipped his hat politely.

"Ah, Mr. Flack. The very person I've been looking for. Could you possibly spare me a moment for a word?"

The publican repressed an impatient sigh. His business might be going to rack and ruin, but he couldn't afford to offend a nob. "Why, certainly, Colonel," he replied with false cordiality. "Though to tell the truth, I'm a bit concerned by the fact that man of yours is behind me bar."

"Shaftoe?" The colonel followed the landlord's gaze, as if the sight were a new one to him. "Making himself useful, is he? Well, I'm glad to see it."

"Wish I could say the same." William Flack came directly to the point. "The fact is, I don't think Mr.

Shaftoe's as interested in helping out as he is in getting on the good side of me daughter."

"Is that so?" Again the colonel feigned surprise. "Well, the sly dog. Can't say as I really blame him, Mr. Flack. Your daughter's a rare beauty."

"Thank you, sir. But to speak plainly, she's all but betrothed to a farmer in these parts. And to speak even plainer still, I expect her to look higher than a valet. So I'd appreciate it if you'd put a flea in your man's ear. Tell him to stay away from my Rosina."

"Well, of course, if that's what you wish. But I think it would be a big mistake. Shaftoe's a rare man, Mr. Flack. Known him all me life. There ain't many like him."

"I'm sure you're right, sir." Mr. Flack's expression didn't quite match the heartiness of his voice. "But like I said, he's not the man for my Rosina. Now what was that matter you wished to discuss with me, sir?"

"Oh yes, that. Oddly enough, it has to do with Shaftoe. I say, could we sit down a bit?" He led the reluctant Flack to a shady spot underneath an elm. "Ah, that's better." The colonel leaned against the trunk while the publican lowered his bulk onto the grass. "Now to get down to brass tacks, sir, I need a businessman's advice. The thing is, my father left a bit of capital to Jem Shaftoe, and I plan to stake him to whatever else it takes to set him up in business. Shaftoe's too ambitious, don't you see, to be content just valeting all his life. Though I must say I'll miss him." He gave a wistful downward glance at the perfection of his oriental-fold cravat. "But I can't begrudge him his opportunities. Especially since he saved my life at Quatre Bras. No, I intend to help him all I can. That's one reason we came to the Hall, actually. To look your village over. Seems Shaftoe set his heart on settling in these parts. He fell in love with—Mitford—when we came through here a few months back."

"And just what sort of business was Mr. Shaftoe thinking of? A tailoring establishment?"

"Oh no. Shaftoe's talents don't run in that direction. He's more like you, if I may say so, Mr. Flack, good at dealing with the public. We're thinking in terms of a posting house."

"Wh-what?"

"A posting house." The colonel raised his voice a bit, as if in doubt of the other's hearing.

There was no problem in that department, but from the way Mr. Flack's face was turning red and his eyes were bulging, there did seem to be some danger of apoplexy.

"You can't be serious!"

"Never more so in my life. I think Shaftoe would make a first-rate publican. Why, just look at the man. As much at home behind the bar as a duck is in the water. The more I think on it, the more I'm convinced that it would be the very thing."

"You're daft—sir! The notion's preposterous. You surely must realize that Mitford's not big enough for two public houses!"

"Now I just happen to think you're wrong there, Mr. Flack. Shaftoe wouldn't be in competition with you, don't you see. No offense, but he was thinking rather bigger than your establishment. Not to take anything away from the Magpie, mind you. It's a capital place, for what it is. And I expect you'll still get the locals at your bar. Village folk are loyal to a fault, don't you agree? But his idea is to have the mail coach make it one of their regular stops. I'm

141

sure I can arrange it. But mostly we'd be depending on the carriage trade. There's a steady stream of gentry traffic that comes through here for Bristol. I'll only have to drop a hint to a few friends here and there, and, well, Shaftoe will soon have more customers than he'll know what to do with."

"Why don't you go on and say it?" Mr. Flack's voice trembled. "What you really plan to do is drive me out of business."

"Oh no, no sir." The colonel looked distressed. "Last thing in the world I'd wish to do. And I know I speak for Shaftoe as well. No, as I said, I'm convinced that a thriving little hamlet like Mitford can accommodate the two of you.

"But of course if you're really worried—" He frowned and seemed to lose himself in thought. "Oh I say, here's an idea." He slapped his thigh as if the proposition had just occurred to him. "Why don't you let Shaftoe buy into the Magpie?"

The landlord quivered like a stricken aspen. "You want me to take that—that—*valet* on as a partner?"

"Maybe it would help if you thought of Shaftoe as a soldier," Colonel Melford offered gently. "A decorated soldier at that."

"I don't care how many bloody decorations he has. I still know blackmail when I hear it."

"Blackmail?" Colonel Sir Rawdon Melford was of a sudden at his haughtiest. "That ugly term hardly applies to the excellent business proposition I've just offered you."

"The devil it don't. I give that little jackanapes a piece of the Magpie, or you drive me out of business. If that ain't blackmail, well I'd like to know what is."

"There's no point in discussing the matter further, I collect, till you're ready to fly down off your high bough and see reason. But I think you're too canny a businessman, Mr. Flack, to let a golden opportunity for expansion pass you by. Tell me the truth, sir. Haven't you ever given the notion of becoming a posting house a thought?" The colonel saw from the fleeting change of expression on the landlord's face that he'd struck a nerve.

"The idea has occurred, of course," Mr. Flack admitted. "But I've never wanted any partner, I'll tell you that much."

"That's because you haven't weighed the pros and cons. Why, there'd be lots of advantages to having a younger man around."

"Well, one of 'em wouldn't be me daughter, if that's the way your mind is working. For even if I should let Mr. Shaftoe buy into the Magpie—and mind you, I ain't saying I'd ever consider it—it would have nothing to do with my Rosina. Like I said before, she's promised."

"Banns been read, have they?"

"No, it ain't gone quite that far yet. But everybody knows she's to wed Joel Holton. And no matter how many posting houses your valet opens, sir, he'll never be half the man young Joel is."

"I think you wouldn't say that if you got to know Jem Shaftoe."

"The thing is, I do know Joel Holton. We're speaking of the man who bowled out Bigham Parish!"

And on that telling verbal blow, the landlord tipped his hat. "Good day, sir." He went striding toward his wooden booth, his face reflecting the war that raged within him. The colonel gazed after him thoughtfully.

# Chapter
# Eighteen

THE MAJORITY OF the Hall residents had been kept waiting for some time now. Indeed the younger members of the party were growing restless and considered walking on ahead.

"Damn silly time to go for a ride," Fawcett grumbled for the second time to the other occupants of the withdrawing room who were either seated or pacing, according to their individual degree of impatience. "It ain't as if he won't be getting any exercise."

"Well, his horse won't, you know," Soame remarked reasonably. "And with the groom having the day off, Rawdon thought he should put Zeus through his paces."

"How many paces does one animal have? It shouldn't take the day. Told him we'd need to leave here by ten. Pretty inconsiderate if you—"

But at that moment Colonel Melford appeared in the doorway and the occupants of the drawing room gave a collective gasp.

"My word! What happened to you?" Lord Fawcett exclaimed.

"My horse tried to jump a stream and didn't quite make it. He stumbled, and I took a spill."

The usually dapper colonel was a mess. The right side of his riding coat and his buckskins, as well as his face, were streaked with mud. His top boots, usually noted for their sheen, were heavily coated. It was all Lady Fawcett could manage not to scold him off the carpet as he moved toward them.

Lord Fawcett did not share this domestic concern. His anxieties went deeper. As he watched his guest's progress, his face grew appalled. "Good God, man, you're limping!"

"Afraid I twisted my ankle rather badly when I fell."

"But you can't have done," his lordship sputtered. "What I mean to say is, of all the days to choose to fall off your horse."

"Yes, I know. Deuced awkward. But it's not as though I could help myself."

While the expressions on other faces ran the gamut from Lord Fawcett's horror to Lady Fawcett's commiseration, Lady Harriet was regarding her ex-fiancé speculatively. "Well you really are slipping, Colonel, if you'll forgive my play on words. I can remember a time when leeches came to you for sticking lessons."

The look he bent upon her was not cordial. "Anybody can have an accident."

"If you say so."

"Look, it's not his riding skill that's at issue here," Lord Fawcett interposed impatiently. "The question is, Rawdon, can you play?"

The colonel took an experimental step and winced pathetically. "Afraid not, old man."

His lordship's groan was heartrending. "Well, there goes the cricket match."

"Oh surely it ain't as bad as all that. There's bound to be someone to take my place."

"Oh come on, Rawdon," Soame Townshend interposed. "Such modesty ill becomes you. You know perfectly well that you're our star. We can't possibly win without you."

"We can't even play without you," Fawcett said glumly. "I had the devil of a time scraping up an eleven as it was. Why, I even had to recruit Squire Tubbs for our long stop, and the man's sixty if he's a day."

"Well, that is a poser. I can't tell you how sorry—oh, but I say!" The colonel struck his forehead. The gesture suggested sudden inspiration—to all but Lady Harriet, that is, who regarded him with narrow-eyed suspicion. "That's it, of course! The very thing. Why didn't I think of it straight off? Shaftoe can take my place."

"Who's Shaftoe?" Selina asked the world in general.

"His valet," Soame explained.

"His valet? In a cricket match? How odd."

"It's worse than odd," her father declared. "It's unthinkable."

"I don't see why," Rawdon replied soothingly. "He's really not at all bad. And he's been practicing me, as you know, so he ought to be in top form. Oh I realize that yours is traditionally a gentrified team—"

"Which traditionally loses," Evelyn Forbes offered, in an aside.

"But if it's a matter of playing or not playing, I

don't think anyone should quibble over class. And, technically, he is of the Hall."

His lordship was obviously weakening.

"Oh really, Aubrey, Rawdon's right, you know," Lady Harriet chimed in to everyone's astonishment, the colonel's most of all. "What would a Maying be without cricket? Shaftoe should be fine."

"It's settled then?"

Fawcett nodded, albeit grudgingly, and Rawdon gave Lady Harriet a grateful look before he limped off to change his clothes and tell Shaftoe, who was already dressed for cricket, that he'd be taking his master's place upon the playing field.

It had been decided that the others would go on ahead and Sir Rawdon would join them after he'd made himself presentable. When he finally rode Zeus (who seemed none the worse for a steed who'd supposedly taken quite a tumble) onto the green-sward, carts and gigs, horses and carriages, and pedestrians of all varieties were arriving from every direction. Stalls dotted the place like giant toad-stools, and raised voices hawked their wares, which included everything from fruit to frippery. A fiddle vied with a ballad singer for the crowd's attention and gained it, only to be preempted by a French-man's troop of dancing dogs.

At first, Rawdon despaired of finding the party from the Hall in all the crush, but then he spied their food tent pitched on a site commanding a good view of the cricket field. He tethered his horse and hobbled toward it.

Selina, Susan, Evelyn, and Soame had deserted the others to go wandering about the green. Lady Fawcett was inside the tent giving the servants last minute instructions before they were turned loose to enjoy themselves until time to serve the cold collation the kitchen had prepared. Lord Fawcett had gone in search of Mr. Flack to inform him of the change in his team's personnel. Lady Harriet was seated at a dining table that had been transported for the occasion. She watched Rawdon's progress with undisguised amusement. Her grin broadened as he collapsed with a stifled groan onto a chair beside her.

"You're really getting much better at this, you know. It's marvelous how your limp has improved since I last saw you."

"But then you always did enjoy my suffering."

"Let's just say I've always appreciated a good performance."

"I'm sure I've no idea of what you're talking about. Not that that's anything new. But be all that as it may, I thank you for putting in a good word for Shaftoe."

"That posed no problem for me. I've always had Shaftoe's best interests at heart."

"Well, at least we're agreed on something. I find that encouraging, don't you?"

"Encouraging? I fail to follow."

They were interrupted then by Lord Fawcett who came beaming toward them. "I say, we've had a real stroke of luck here, Rawdon. Flack's just told me there's a gentleman staying at the Magpie who's a regular cricket wizard. He can take your place. Flack's gone to fetch him."

They watched the two men approach across the green, while the colonel struggled to suppress a string of oaths and Lady Harriet quoted, for no apparent reason, "The best laid schemes o' mice and men gang aft a-gley."

The landlord presented his guest, then hurried away to deal with some new crisis. Fawcett looked the major over, obviously pleased with what he saw. "I expect Flack told you that we're short one of our eleven. He tells me you're quite a cricketer."

"Well I have played a bit, your lordship." The major smiled modestly. "And I don't mind saying there's nothing I enjoy more."

"Good. Then it's settled. You'll join our team."

"I am sorry, sir." Indeed the gentleman looked quite crestfallen. "But I fear that's impossible. Thought I'd come and explain myself in person, don't you see. Seemed most ungracious just to send my excuses after your graciously expressed interest. For I'd be quite honored, your lordship, under other circumstances, don't you know."

It was taking all Sir Rawdon's self-restraint not to interrupt the flow and tell the fellow to come to the point. Not only was he a dandified toadeater, he was also too prosy by half. What's more, the colonel didn't care much for the way the cove kept stealing glances at Harriet, who was looking altogether too fetching in a muslin round dress topped by an emerald green spencer, with a bonnet to match.

Lord Fawcett seemed to share the colonel's impatience. "Are you saying that you don't wish to play, sir?"

"Oh no. No indeed. Begging your lordship's pardon, I'm not saying that. In truth, there's nothing I could wish for more. The sad truth is, I can't play. Bad shoulder, don't you know. Can scarcely lift my bowling arm without wincing. Impossible to bat as well."

"Oh what a shame." Lady Harriet's face was a

study in sympathy. "Tell me, Major, did you fall off your horse?"

There was a moment's hesitation. "Why, yes, as a matter of fact, I did take a spill."

"Oh indeed? There does seem to be a lot of that happening lately."

"Mine is an old injury, your ladyship."

"I see. And were you, like Colonel Melford here, in the cavalry?"

"No, Lady Harriet. I was in the Fortieth Foot."

"I can't tell you how relieved I am to hear it. Somehow the picture of our mounted troops constantly tumbling off their chargers is quite unnerving. Thank goodness the Corsican monster is now under control."

Major Mortram was looking a bit out of his depth.

"Pay her no mind," Colonel Melford advised. "Lady Harriet is known for her odd sense of humor."

"Oh blast!" Lord Fawcett muttered to himself more than to the company. "This leaves us right back where we were."

"I am sorry." The major looked contrite. "There's nothing I'd rather do—"

"Quite," Lord Fawcett cut him short. And then, as if to atone for such incivility, "Won't you join us for a glass of wine, sir?" he asked, nodding to the decanter and glasses a servant had placed upon the table. "But pray excuse me. I'd best go round up our team and have a word with 'em. Especially the valet." He seemed to choke upon the term. "You're sure then, Rawdon, that he should bowl?"

"Positive."

"Well, it ain't as if we've got a lot of choice. Send Soame and Evelyn over when they get back, will you? Told 'em not to go wandering off."

The others watched his receding back in silence for a moment, then Rawdon limped around the table to pour claret into delicate crystal glasses. "Poor Fawcett," Lady Harriet sighed as she accepted hers. "He really does seem to take this whole business hard."

"Don't see why." Rawdon reluctantly handed a glass to the major. "They keep saying the Hall's never won."

"Oh yes, but they had such high hopes of you. Did you know, Major Mortram, that the colonel here is a nonesuch when it comes to cricket?"

"Oh is that so? Pity about the leg then."

"Ankle, actually."

Harriet shook her head sadly. "And a pity about your arm, Major."

"Shoulder, ma'am."

"Whatever. Do you know, it boggles the mind to think what this day might have been if you two gentlemen were hale and hearty. Cricket history could have been made in Mitford."

"Oh I'm sure you exaggerate, Lady Harriet."

"And I'm sure she's bamming you, Major Mortram." The colonel took an ungenteel gulp of claret.

"I understand that you're on a sightseeing junket." Harriet smiled warmly at the newcomer. "Tell me, sir, what is your impression of Berkshire?"

Rawdon listened glumly while Mortram rhapsodized over the local scenery. The cove, he noted, did seem to have a special feel for the flora and fauna, Harriet's ruling passion, that Rawdon himself had never really been able to share. Oh he knew a rose from a violet, that sort of thing; but the major appeared to be on speaking terms with all sorts of esoteric plant life, even giving them their Latin names, by God. And Harriet was lapping the conversation up.

It occurred to Rawdon to wonder if Major Mortram had intentionally boned up on the subject. Still, he'd have had no way of knowing he'd be meeting Harriet. It was just that the cursed fellow was too fly by half.

"Oh I say, Major." He interrupted a discussion of oxlips, arums, and heartsease to barge into the conversation. "You're in the Fortieth Foot I understand."

"No longer, sir. I sold out."

"I see. Well then, you probably know my good friend George Lincoln."

"That would be *Colonel* Lincoln?"

"By this time I expect so. *Major* last time I heard. Promoted in the field then, was he?"

"That's right. A regular lionheart he was, as I collect you know."

"Knew him well then, did you?"

"Alas no. Mostly by reputation."

"I see." Rawdon lapsed back into his reverie, while the naturalists took up their conversation where he'd interrupted it.

He congratulated himself upon establishing so easily what he'd only suspected. 'Major' Mortram had never been near the 40th Foot. He didn't know George Lincoln, either personally or by reputation, since the field-promoted colonel was purely a figment of Rawdon's imagination.

What wasn't so simple to figure was just what sort of game the cove was playing. He certainly had Harry eating out of his hand. Rawdon couldn't recall when she'd been so animated. And all over a variety of wild primrose? The notion was ludicrous. No, if

152

Harry was looking like a sixteen-year-old, it was because the attentive major was charming the eye-teeth right out of her head. The question was, why?

From the very first, he'd labeled Mortram a fortune hunter. God knows, he was well equipped to do the job. Rawdon skimmed the handsome features with a jaundiced eye. But Harry was no proper target for the major's talents. It was common knowledge she hadn't a feather left to fly with. Practice perhaps? That was more acceptable in Rawdon's mind than a niggling suspicion that the spurious soldier might actually be falling in love with Lady Harriet. That condition was, after all, one which he himself was well qualified to recognize. He was relieved just then to see their wandering foursome approaching. It was more than time to interrupt this tête-à-tête.

Rawdon's eyes narrowed as he watched Harriet introduce Major Mortram to the other members of their party. Susan appeared ready to sink. The major gave no sign, however, that he'd ever seen Miss Tunstall before. Nor did Selina betray any previous acquaintanceship. Evelyn Forbes was no dissembler, though. The look he bent upon the major was suspicious; his nod was curt. Soame Townshend, as usual, was the soul of affability, welcoming Mortram to the festivities as if he were Master of the Revels himself.

Lady Harriet dutifully repeated Lord Fawcett's message, but the cricket players were in no hurry to take the field. "The other team always keeps us waiting anyhow," Evelyn told them, as he accepted a glass of wine.

"Why would they do a thing like that?" Soame asked.

"Really couldn't say. A chance to put their betters in their place, perhaps."

Lady Fawcett, who was looking a bit harried, emerged from the refreshment tent just then and joined them thankfully. Never again would she plan a ball for the day following a Maying, she confided. After Major Mortram (who Rawdon noted was stuck to their party like sealing wax) had been presented to her ladyship, Selina seemed struck by a sudden thought. "Oh, Mariana, you really must invite the major to Papa's birthday ball. He's a stranger here in Mitford, you know."

It was a contest between Rawdon Melford and Evelyn Forbes as to which thought less of this notion. Lady Fawcett, however, was more than eager to please her stepdaughter, and the invitation was graciously extended.

"Pity about the cricket and your shoulder, Major," Rawdon remarked pointedly, "but don't let us detain you. I'm sure you must have other things to do."

His rudeness seemed to shock the rest of the company; the major, however, didn't turn a hair. "That's the joy of being a tourist. My time is quite my own."

"Why then, you must join our party," Lady Fawcett said hastily. "We have the best possible view of the playing field, and we'll be picnicking after the match."

Major Mortram expressed his delight at the invitation and shifted his chair to face the field where some players were now beginning to gather. The stratagem brought him even closer to Lady Harriet. Rawdon rose and poured himself more claret. "Mind your limp," Harriet whispered, and earned a setdown look.

She was enjoying the situation immensely. She'd

never seen the cocksure colonel quite so out of sorts. She would not have dreamed she had the power to make him jealous. The discovery had gone straight to her head. "What's sauce for the goose," and other similar adages kept flitting through her mind.

Besides the pleasures of putting Rawdon in a pet, Harriet was forced to admit that she was enjoying the attention of the handsome stranger. It had been a long time since anyone had paid her court. Not since she'd lost her fortune, to be precise. Harriet was far too levelheaded not to suspect the major's motives. Her best guess was that they involved Selina and Susan in some way. But she decided to lay her suspicions aside for the time being and just enjoy the day.

Evelyn Forbes was not nearly so ready to abandon his suspicions. They were, in fact, growing by leaps and bounds. He thought it high time to find out for himself just what was what. "Come take a walk with me," he whispered to Selina.

"A walk?" She didn't bother to lower her voice. "Whatever for? We've already tramped every square inch of the green. I'm worn out. Besides, you're due on the playing field. Papa keeps staring this way."

"That's just it," he improvised as the smell of gingerbread wafted his way from the nearest booth. "I want to get something to sustain me through the match."

"For heaven's sake, Evelyn, can't you think of anything but eating? You've already had two buns and a jam tart. I should think that would keep you from fainting away with hunger. If not, go raid the tent." She gestured behind them. "There's tons of food in there."

"Selina, come on!" he said between his teeth as he

extended a hand and practically jerked her from her chair.

"Oh very well," she replied ungraciously, given little choice.

He walked her rapidly toward the gingerbread, but instead of buying, he steered her around the booth and out of sight. "All right, Selina. I want to know what's going on here."

"Whatever do you mean?" Her eyes widened.

"Don't play the innocent with me. I've known you far too long. You know damn well what I'm talking about. Just what sort of game are you and that cove playing?"

"What cove?"

"The major. If he is one."

"Have you lost your mind entirely? That gentleman and I weren't playing any game. I've not exchanged two words with him. No, I'm a liar. Let's make that four. I do believe I said 'How do you do?' Did I add 'sir'? That would bring my part of the exchange up to five."

"Your sarcasm's wasted." Passersby were looking at them curiously, but the intent twosome hardly noticed. "I've seen that fellow everywhere I look for the past several days. And if he's in these parts to admire the scenery, then I'm a Dutchman. It's my guess it's no coincidence he arrived here right after you returned home. And you may have only exchanged five words today, but I saw you talking to him yesterday at the May House."

"I did no such thing."

"Can't look me in the eye and say that, can you? You always were a pitiful liar, Selina."

"And you always were a snoop. If I did speak to Major Mortram, just what business is it of yours?"

"I collect I've known your family long enough to feel obligated not to let you make a cake out of yourself. And I'll tell you right now, old girl, there's something fishy about your major."

"He's not my major. And you're being absurd." She studied his face carefully. "Why, Evelyn, I do believe you're jealous," she crowed.

"Of that pretty coxcomb? Don't be daft. The thing is, I know the type."

"You know the type!" she mocked. "Well, well, well. I defer to your vast experience of the world, Mr. Forbes."

"You don't have to leave Berkshire to recognize a Jack Sharp, Selina. And if you don't tell me what you're up to, by God, I'll speak to your father."

"You wouldn't!"

"Oh no? Just watch me." He turned as if to go, but Selina grabbed his sleeve.

"You mustn't speak to Papa, Evelyn. You've got it all wrong, you know. Oh don't look like that. I don't mean *all* wrong, exactly. What I'm trying to say is, it's not me he followed here. It's Susan."

"Susan!" He looked stunned.

"Yes, Susan. So you see there's no need for you to speak to Papa."

"Oh isn't there?" he asked grimly. "I knew Susan had to be involved. But she always seemed so upset at the sight of the fellow that I thought she was worried about you. A clandestine romance seems more your line of country."

"Well, it really isn't Susan's sort of thing," Selina admitted candidly. "You're right there, Evelyn. She hates sneaking around. But she has no choice, don't you see. Her mother's forbidden her to see the major."

"For good reason, I'll wager."

"No, not a bit of it. It's simply prejudice on her mother's part. She thinks everyone who even looks at her daughter is a fortune hunter. And it simply isn't fair. Major Mortram can't be blamed because his father squandered away the family fortune. And his antecedents are impeccable. He's cousin to an earl."

"Told you that, did he?"

"Well, he had to defend himself from those accusations, didn't he? Oh Evelyn," her eyes glowed, "it's the most romantic thing. We visited the Assembly Rooms in Susan's village, and there was this incredibly handsome man who couldn't take his eyes off her all evening long. And, of course, it wasn't possible for him to be introduced."

"Why not, pray?"

"Oh, you know what self-important tyrants village masters of ceremonies can be. But the major and his partner stood up next to Susan and her partner in the country dance, and he whispered an invitation to meet him the next day."

"And she agreed?" Evelyn looked shocked.

"She wasn't going to go at first, but I talked her into it."

"You would."

"Well somebody had to. Susan's my dearest friend, but she really is fainthearted. And, really, there was nothing at all scandalous in the assignation, so you needn't look so Friday-faced. They met in a public library, for heaven's sake! And naturally, I went along. And, oh Evelyn, you should have seen the two of them. It had been love at first sight on the major's part. And, well, he quite swept Susan off her feet."

"In love with him, is she?" His face was expressionless.

"Of course. You've seen him. He looks like a Greek god. Could you blame her?"

He let that pass. "And she doesn't mind, I suppose, that he's dangling after Lady Harriet this very minute?"

"Of course not." She looked scornful. "That's merely to throw people off the scent. He's not interested in Harriet. Why, she's an ancient."

"She ain't all that long in the tooth. And she is a beauty. But of course," he added deliberately, "she doesn't have a fortune. So I expect you're right."

"That was a caddish thing to say, Evelyn. You've absolutely no basis for judging Major Mortram. It's nothing but prejudice on your part. Please, please, promise me you won't speak to Papa."

"Very well. I promise."

"Oh, Evelyn, you are a brick." She hugged him impulsively. "I knew you couldn't let Papa wreck Susan's happiness."

"Actually, Selina, I never had any intention of speaking to his lordship. I do mean to put a flea in Colonel Melford's ear, though. After all, he's Susan's guardian."

"Evelyn, you—you—traitor. You mustn't. I'll never forgive you if you do. And Susan will never forgive you."

It did occur then to Mr. Forbes that his interference might put him in an untenable position where Miss Tunstall was concerned. Lady Selina saw him begin to waver and pressed home her advantage.

"I tell you what, Evelyn. Simply promise me you won't take any hasty action. For you're quite wrong

159

about Major Mortram. You really are. So at least take a bit of time to get to know him." She was suddenly inspired. "It really would be a shame, you know, to put a damper on Papa's birthday ball. At least wait till that's over, and if you're still convinced that you should take some action, well, that's between you and your conscience," she concluded virtuously.

Evelyn eyed his old friend suspiciously. It was unlike Selina to be so reasonable. Still, the ball was little more than twenty-four hours away. What harm would that do? Besides, he had a cricket match to play.

"Very well then." He gave in grudgingly. "But don't think I'm going to change my mind, Selina. I know a wrong 'un when I see one. The day after the ball I'm having a word with Colonel Melford."

"Agreed. For if you must, you must."

Selina strove not to look triumphant.

# Chapter
# Nineteen

J EM SHAFTOE APPROACHED the cricket ground with more trepidation than he'd felt on the field of Waterloo. There, at least, he'd had the camaraderie of his fellow rankers. Here, his status as an interloper was all too apparent.

Lord Fawcett had presented him to his teammates with so little explanation that it was obvious they'd been forewarned. Their response was polite, but chilly. As for their opponents, amusement vied with scorn on most of those faces. I'll wipe off that smirk before the afternoon's over, the valet promised himself silently, as he took note of Farmer Holton's expression.

It wasn't the players, though, that Shaftoe found most disconcerting. It was the gallery. He'd played a lot of cricket in his time, but mostly of the regimental variety where the spectators had been soldiers with a sprinkling of wives and camp followers mixed in. So he was keenly conscious of the party from the Hall, who were moving their chairs a bit nearer to the field. He knew that the colonel, in spite of his ho-hum attitude, was nervous for him, realizing how much he had riding on the match. He was aware of the astonishment of the Hall servants who, one by one, were spotting him there among his betters in the field. He registered Landlord William Flack's contempt, and this was of no particular concern. For he could, he knew, put all of these people out of his mind with minimum difficulty. The primary concern of his present trepidation was the girl with the flashing black eyes and roses on her bonnet: Miss Rosina Flack.

She'd been direct and to the point when he'd informed her he was going to play. "Are ye daft? Don't do it."

"And why ever not?"

"Because Joel Holton will make mincemeat of you, that's why."

"Perhaps."

"No perhaps about it. It's sure as houses. Why, Joel's the best bowler in these parts, and that's by a long shot. And the Mitford team's exactly that—a team. Why, they play together all the time. Successfully. And as for that gaggle of gentlemen from the Hall, tell me, has that lot even practiced?" She paused, and he reluctantly shook his head. "See what I mean? This whole business is naught but a joke."

"Well, then, I expect you'll be joining in the laughter."

"Maybe that's just what I'd rather not do. Don't play, Jem. Papa's down on you enough without adding this in. Cricket's his passion, as I expect you know."

He should have been glad, he supposed afterward, that she cared enough to wish him to save face. He wasn't.

"You've a pretty poor opinion of my manhood, haven't you, Rosina Flack?" he'd challenged.

"Well, now I wouldn't go quite so far as to say that," she'd winked, recalling the times he'd kissed her.

But he was having none of this flirtatiousness. "You're just like everybody else. You judge a man by the sheer bulk of him, never mind what he's made up of. Well, that may do for oxen, but you don't measure a man just by inches and stone."

"Did I say anything about the size of you?" she'd flared back. "I merely pointed out that if you play today, Joel will make mincemeat of you. He's been dying for the chance. You surely must know that. And here you go offering up yourself on a silver platter."

"You've just made my point, Miss Flack," he'd replied frigidly. "You're a much better judge of an ox than you are of a man."

He'd bowed then and had gone striding off to join the other players. Now he was all too conscious of her, seated beside her father on the grass, holding her parasol against the sun. And he wished he'd not been quite so cocky.

Shaftoe had been dead right about one thing, the colonel was nervous indeed. What had seemed a stroke of genius earlier now seemed the sheerest folly. There must have been better schemes for helping his valet win the woman of his choice without having him go head to head with the redoubtable Joel Holton. Rawdon eyed the farmer gloomily as he warmed up his arm. Not only was his skill well known, but the confidence of the fellow was all too apparent.

"A pretty motley crew, wouldn't you say?"

It spoke volumes for the colonel's preoccupation that he'd almost forgotten that Harriet was beside him. When they'd shifted their positions to watch the match, it had taken some swift maneuvering on his part to bring this happy state of affairs about. But Major Mortram, far from being outmaneuvered, had attached himself to her other side and engaged her in a conversation that had treated the colonel to her back. This exclusion, plus his concern for Shaftoe's venture into the cricket lists, had focused his attention on the field. "Eh?" He snapped to now, and encountered Harriet's amused expression. "A motley crew? Their side, you mean?"

"No, ours. Just look at them."

"I have been. They look all right, I'd say."

"No, they don't. Take the way they're dressed, for one thing—those shirt points and stiff cravats, those coats with pinched-in waists. They've no freedom of movement whatsoever."

"Well I expect they'll take off their coats. Shaftoe will, at any rate."

"Even so, these gentlemen cricketers, by very definition, are quite out of their depth."

"That's a slanderous thing to say." He looked at her coldly. "Have you gone republican since you lost your money, Harry?"

"Not a bit of it. I'm just stating the obvious. Look at the opposition, won't you. Note what they're wearing."

"Smocks, loose shirts, in the main. Oh well, I take your point. If you'll pardon me, I'll go ask the umpire to have everybody strip. Fair's fair."

"Don't get on your high ropes with me, Rawdon. I'm just trying to point out that while class distinction as a rule tips in our favor, this time the balance goes the other way. Look at the men they have out there. You know all about Farmer Holton. Working in the field all day keeps him in the peak of athletic condition, wouldn't you say?" She paused, but got no response. "Then there are two blacksmiths yonder. Note the muscles. There's a day laborer—also quite fit—three more farm lads—"

"Don't forget the rat catcher," he interrupted. "What's your point, Harry?"

"Isn't it obvious? I think you should be out there with your own kind instead of offering up poor Shaftoe as a living sacrifice. If you had to finagle him onto the field, why didn't you place him on the winning side?"

He chose to ignore the fact that she seemed well aware of all his scheming and took umbrage at her premise instead. "Aren't you being a bit hard on the Hall? Granted our coves may not be as burly as the blacksmiths and the farmers. But cricket's not all brawn, you know. It's a game of skill. I can't speak for the entire field," he looked with a sinking sensation at the ten gentlemen and Shaftoe gathered together for a last-minute rally, "I can only speak for the coves from the Hall. But I understand that young Forbes can hold his own, and I know for a fact that Fawcett and Soame Townshend both played for their schools."

Harriet laughed. "And they've retained about as much of that ability as they remember of their Greek and Latin, I daresay. And in addition to them we have a curate, a doctor, and a smattering of country squires."

"Would you care to wager on the outcome?"

"Don't be absurd. The outcome's inevitable."

"So you say. But how about a little flutter to make the thing more interesting?"

"You know my opinion of gambling."

"Even on a sure thing? I shouldn't think you'd consider that gambling."

"Well, then, let's just say I don't wish to take your money. Nor would it be ethical to wager, even on a sure thing, with no way to back it up."

"Oh I wasn't thinking of money."

"What then?" She stared at him suspiciously.

"If I win, you'll save all your dances for me tomorrow night."

"I can't do that."

"Oh come on, Harry. Surely at our ages we don't have to abide by that fusty 'only two consecutive dances' rule. That's for the infantry."

"You may be right, but the fact of the matter is I'm already promised to Major Mortram for the prescribed two dances. I daresay he might have asked for more if he'd realized what an ancient I am." She tossed her head and turned her back.

"Damnation." The colonel cursed himself beneath his breath for his clumsiness, then focused his attention once more upon the field. The coin had just been tossed and the team from the Hall had won the bat.

It seemed at first that the gentlemen cricketers were determined to live up to Lady Harriet's direst predictions. The curate was first to defend his wicket and it was probable that the saintly man had never before encountered such a look of scorn as the bowler, Farmer Holton, bent upon him. He was bowled out without a stroke from sheer nervousness.

The squire who followed fared no better. The balls were sent flying off his stumps. There was a collective sigh of relief when the farmer had completed his six balls, a maiden over.

Things improved somewhat with the other bowler. Evelyn Forbes managed to back stroke a pitch that landed at his feet. But, alas, due to a fieldsman with a powerful arm, he was bowled out. But then Lord Fawcett's bat connected with a slow lob, and he beat the return to the stumps, much to his bride's delight. Indeed, Lady Fawcett quite forgot herself and cheered so lustily that her huzzahs reached her spouse's ears, which turned quite pink with pleasure.

After that, Soame Townshend strolled nonchalantly over to pick up his bat and score three notches off his hit to everyone's amazement, especially his own.

When it finally came Shaftoe's turn to defend his wicket, Colonel Rawdon Melford put his head in his hands and groaned. It was the valet's bad luck to face the bulletlike bowling of his rival for the landlord's daughter's hand.

The enmity the curate had seen in the farmer's eyes was nothing when compared to the naked hatred now directed at Jem Shaftoe. Hatred mingled with unholy anticipation. Just so might the operator of the guillotine have looked at poor King Louis before the knife blade dropped. Holton prolonged the moment to savor it. He threw a glance back over his shoulder to make sure the landlord's daughter's eyes were fixed upon him. They were. Along with those of every other breath-holding spectator on the green.

"Bowl, you bastard," Shaftoe muttered between clinched teeth. The farmer's lip curled in a snarl. He coiled like a spring, sprinted, and then delivered. The blurred ball whistled like a bullet toward the stumps. There came an ear-splitting crack and the missile went sailing fullpitch over the boundary—a six run for the valet.

The age of miracles had indeed arrived. After Shaftoe's coup, his team took heart. One of the country squires made a good hit on the second bowler's slow pitch and the runners for the Hall sprinted back and forth. The village fieldsman became so rattled by all the pandemonium from the gallery that when he finally did retrieve the ball, he threw it wildly, and the squire was able to score another notch before it reached the stumps.

It was said afterward that there had never been such a cricket game at any Maying. When five hours were up—an interval of time that most declared seemed like mere minutes—the Hall team was victor over the village by a scant two points. And there was no doubt at all as to who had been the hero of the day. Not only had Jem Shaftoe been responsible for the lion's share of his team's impressive total, he had bowled out the mighty Farmer Holton, a thing heretofore unheard of. What's more, at the conclusion of the match, that poor sport had responded to his humiliation by hurling the ball at the ground with such velocity that it had actually buried itself. And there was not a soul around who did not realize that the farmer wished the target might have been Jem Shaftoe's head.

The valet was hoisted to the shoulders of his gentlemen teammates, amid the clamorous cheers of the spectators, where a spirit of fair play and a love for the game of cricket outdid their previous partisanship. But as the triumphant procession left the grounds, there was only one accolade the hero was interested in. His eyes searched out and found Miss

Flack's. She was standing quietly amid the hubbub, and the smile she gave him was as enigmatic as any ever painted by Leonardo.

First, he had to wade through all the backslapping and congratulations of the servant's hall. For now it seemed that the newcomer was really one of them. Their own status had been somehow enhanced by his achievement. Then, when he finally was allowed to make his way to Rosina's side, it was only to be intercepted by her father who pumped his arm vigorously up and down with both hands as though drawing water. "My boy, my boy! I'd no idea!" The landlord was misty eyed. "What a performance. You'll go down in Mitford history, you will. Really, I'd no idea. No notion whatsoever. And as concerns that business proposition the colonel was discussing—well, anytime you're ready to talk about it, you know where to find me." Mr. Flack pumped the valet's hand a few more times, just for good measure. "But now I collect you've other things on your mind, eh?" And he gave a significant nod Rosina's way before hurrying off to open up his booth for the benefit of the parched players and thirsty onlookers.

Mr. Shaftoe and Miss Flack stood for the longest time merely looking at each other. "Quite the little hero, ain't you?" she finally said.

"Well, now, I guess that all depends."

"I'd call it a fact. You certainly sent Joel Holton home with his tail between his legs."

"I won't say I didn't enjoy that, but you know as well as I do that that's not what this is all about."

"Oh do I?" She tossed her head, sending the black curls bouncing beneath her rose-trimmed bonnet. "It seems to me I'm about the last person around to know what's going on. Take that conversation you

169

just had with my father, for instance. Mind telling me what that was all about?"

"Oh, just a business proposition. I'm thinking of buying into the Magpie."

"So that's it, is it. You knew that the proper way to worm yourself into Papa's good graces was to be a cricket nonesuch. Regular Machiavelli, ain't you? I don't doubt that's why you came to Mitford in the first place, Mr. Shaftoe. To find a well-established public house like the Magpie."

"I came to Mitford in the first place by pure accident. But I came back because of a black-eyed, heartless wench who's far too flirtatious for her own good. Oh I've always wanted me own establishment, I don't mind admitting. But I wouldn't have necessarily picked out Mitford as the Eden of the world."

"Well, now, just where you set up is your own affair, Mr. Shaftoe. Just as long as you don't make the mistake of thinking a partnership in the Magpie automatically includes me."

"That being the case, then, I'm not interested."

"Not much of a businessman, are you?"

"Good enough to know it's you I'd best negotiate with before I go talking to your papa." His eyes gleamed as he moved toward her.

"Now you look here, Jem Shaftoe," she protested, backing away. "You get that daft notion out of your head. You are not going to kiss me with the whole blessed parish looking on."

"Oh, you think not?" And with the same, quick decisiveness that had bowled out Joel Holton, he pulled Rosina to his chest and kissed her long and ardently to the accompaniment of widely scattered titters, a few whistles, and even a smattering of applause.

Rawdon Melford watched his man's maneuver. A wide grin split his face. He was seated with the other residents of the Hall and their guests—which included most of the triumphant team—before a cold collation dominated by an enormous round of beef. He had managed to seat himself by Lady Harriet once again, but once again she was being monopolized by Major Mortram. She did, however, glance his way in time to see the grin. Her eyes traveled in the direction he was looking just as Shaftoe reluctantly released Miss Flack.

"Well, well, your little scheme worked, I see," she said in a low aside. "You can stop limping now."

"Oh I have already. I was miraculously cured when Shaftoe bowled the farmer out. Pity you were too cowardly to bet. Your pathetic gentlemen players didn't do too badly. Now admit it."

"*Shaftoe* didn't do too badly. I can't help but wonder what the result might have been if you had played instead." She delivered this Parthian shot as Major Mortram claimed her attention once again.

Even though it was generally acknowledged that had it not been for the valet their team would have met the fate of previous years, there was still enough glory left to spread around among the cricket players from the Hall. Lady Selina's eyes were shining as she complimented Mr. Townshend on his play. And Miss Susan Tunstall, seated as far as possible from Major Mortram, and for the moment oblivious of his presence, gave Mr. Evelyn Forbes her sincere opinion that he would be right at home at Lords, playing for five hundred guineas to each side. As soon as they could do so without appearing too rag mannered, the foursome excused itself to go visit the booths, watch the games of quoits and bowls and ninepins, and eventually wind up among the throng collected in front of the May House, where the band had just struck up a tune. There, they eagerly joined in the country dance that was being set afloat, country lads and lasses at the bottom of the set with the ladies and gentlemen at the top.

The other members of the cricket team soon followed their example and left the feast to go explore the fair. Lady Harriet and Major Mortram, however, seemed oblivious to this general exodus and continued in animated conversation, while Colonel Melford stared glumly off into space. Lord Fawcett, having unsuccessfully wished them all three to Jericho, picked up his glass of claret, left his place at the head of the table, and joined his wife who was isolated at the other end.

"I heard you cheering for me," he murmured softly.

She turned pink. "Did you? Oh dear. I'm afraid I made quite a spectacle of myself. But, oh Aubrey, you were truly magnificent."

"Simply lucky, that's all," he replied modestly, though he did look enormously pleased all the same.

"Aubrey," she reached over and placed her hand timidly upon his. "Can you ever forgive me?" she whispered.

"Forgive you?" His eyes widened. "Whatever for?"

"F-for being so stupid, I suppose. I seem to have botched everything since we've come home. But I'm learning. I truly am. Oh, I know I'll never be able to run things as smoothly as the first Lady Fawcett. But I will make you comfortable, you'll see."

Fawcett opened his mouth to protest, but she rushed on before her courage failed her. "And about tomorrow night—I should have known you'd hate the notion of a birthday ball, but the thing is, you see, Aubrey, you're so very special to me that I wished for the whole world to honor the occasion. It was positively birdwitted of me not to have consulted your feelings on the matter, and I promise never to do so again. Can you forgive me?"

"Forgive you?" he said huskily. "There's nothing to forgive. I'm the one who's been acting like an ass. The truth is, Mariana, I've not been able to deal with turning forty. Here I am with a beautiful, young bride, and I suddenly felt—antiquated."

"How ridiculous." Her voice rose indignantly. "Why you're a young man, Aubrey. One only had to watch you on the cricket field to know that. That, plus other things." She blushed becomingly.

He broke into a broad smile, his first in days. "I really didn't do too badly, did I?" he agreed. "I say," he looked furtively down the table at the threesome who were paying them no mind, "do you think we could slip away, back to the Hall?" he whispered. "We haven't—been alone together—for ages."

"I don't see why not." Her heart was in her eyes.

"Remember what the gypsy told us about a son?"

"Oh yes. I'd like that above all things."

"And so would I."

"Do you think there was any truth in her prophecy, Aubrey?"

"I've no idea." He took her by the hand and drew her up. "But come on," he said. "Let's go find out."

The strains of the band were floating across the greensward to reach the Fawcett table. "Would you care to dance, Harry?" Colonel Melford rudely interrupted one of Major Mortram's anecdotes.

"Why no thank you, Colonel," she answered formally. "I wouldn't dream of putting your poor ankle in jeopardy." She glanced down the table and saw Lord and Lady Fawcett rising to their feet. "Goodness, our hosts are leaving. I really should go, too. Mariana may need my help for some last-minute preparations at the Hall."

"Don't be such a ninnyhammer," the colonel replied shortly. "Lady Fawcett needs no help from you."

"Oh?" She took a second look at the newlyweds and appeared embarrassed. "Well yes. I do see what you mean."

The trio watched in silence while their host and hostess left them, hand in hand, with their hearts in their eyes, and without so much as a nod of farewell in their guests' direction.

# Chapter
# Twenty

SHAFTOE WHISTLED SOFTLY between his teeth as he delicately applied pomade to Colonel Melford's hair.

"Go easy with that stuff, will you? I've no desire to look like a damned Frenchie."

"Just trying to make the most of your crowning glory, sir. Don't think you realize just how lucky you are. You could be sleeping in curl papers like Lord Byron, you know."

"Not bloody likely," the other snorted in contempt. He eyed his black curls, reflected in the glass, with a jaundiced eye. Shaftoe resumed his whistling as he picked up a starched cravat. "And do you have to be so damned cheerful?"

The whistling stopped. "Sorry, sir. I wasn't aware of my behavior."

"Oh blast! I'm the one who's sorry," the other sighed. "Go ahead, whistle. Dance a jig if you will. God knows you've every right, and I should be congratulating you instead of snapping your head off. Don't know what's put me in such a foul mood, but there it is."

"Yes, sir." There was a period of silence while Shaftoe arranged the cravat with deft fingers. The colonel looked approvingly at the completed trone d'amour. "You know, you could be wasting yourself behind the bar." He stood while Shaftoe helped him shrug into his black evening coat, made, of course, by Weston. There had been no need for the excessive padding that this fashionable tailor at times resorted to. The colonel's own broad shoulders took care of that detail. Shaftoe stood back to assess his handiwork and, as always, felt a slight stab of envy for the aristocrat's tall, muscular physique.

The colonel was also regarding himself in the cheval glass, but with none of the same appreciation. Indeed, he looked down right dissatisfied.

"Anything wrong, sir?" Shaftoe whipped out a clothes brush and applied it to the impeccable black material.

"Here now, that's enough of that. I'll do, I suppose." The colonel turned away from his reflection and crossed the room to the desk where he pulled out two cigars. He flipped one Shaftoe's way. "Tell me, Jem," he inquired casually when both cheroots were going, "what exactly did that old hag tell you?"

Shaftoe looked bemused for just a moment. "Oh." His face had become enlightened. "You mean the gypsy."

"Of course. She read your palm down in the servants' hall, didn't she?"

"That's right."

"Well then, what did she say?"

Shaftoe laughed. "She said I'd be starting a new venture and marrying a black-eyed wench who fancied herself in love with someone else but who'd discover she was in love with me."

"Well she certainly got that right," the colonel observed gloomily.

"Well, why wouldn't she have done? What with you coaching her."

"Well, did she tell you anything else, Jem? Anything I couldn't have told her about, I mean."

The valet wrinkled his brow in thought. "Not as I recall, sir. That was pretty much it."

"Hmmm. Then tell me. You're a pretty shrewd sort of fellow. Do you think there's anything to that sort of thing? Telling fortunes, I mean."

"No, sir." The other spoke firmly. "I think it's simply a matter of picking up bits of information, which in our gypsy's case you supplied, plus a lot of educated guesses. Then, too," he reflected, "I expect they learn to read character and just call it reading palms."

"Hmmm. I agree with you, of course, except . . ."

"Yes, sir?" the valet prompted.

"Well, it still leaves a few things unexplained. 'More things in heaven and earth, Horatio, than are dreamed of in your philosophy,' and all that rot. There was the matter of the pink waistcoat, remember?"

"Oh yes. The one Mr. Townshend was wearing. I'll grant you, sir, that's a poser. But on the other hand, the gypsy said that Miss Tunstall would marry the man wearing it, and that seems rather unlikely. It appears that Mr. Townshend's interests are directed more toward Lady Selina. The odds are running in the servants' hall that those two will make a match of it."

"Are they now?" The colonel's eyebrows rose. "Well, I must say, Selina's seemed greatly improved since Soame's arrival. Civil all around, even to her father's wife. But still," he lapsed back into his morose mood, "it's early days yet. Soame could still wind up wedded to Susan."

"Anything's possible, of course. But I wouldn't take the old hag too seriously if I were you, sir."

"No, I suppose not. Still—" The colonel extinguished his cigar and said almost too casually, "There's one other odd thing she said that I sure as hell didn't prime her with."

"Oh? And what was that, sir?" Shaftoe was reapplying the clothes brush, post cigar.

"I didn't tell her that Harriet would meet any tall, handsome stranger. She came up with that bit on her own."

"Well, gypsies always provide females with tall, handsome strangers," the valet replied diplomatically. "It's considered part of the package."

"Yes, but those tall, handsome strangers don't usually appear. But here's this so-called Major Mortram fawning all over Harry, and she's lapping it all up like a kitten with its first taste of cream. Damned if I can figure the whole thing out. We had him pegged dead to rights as a fortune hunter while he was dangling after my godchild. But Harry's the proverbial church mouse. There's no two ways about it, the fellow's fallen for her."

Shaftoe opened his mouth to explain the situation, but then thought better of it. His and Sir Rawdon's lives had been linked since they were children; they'd been together through the proverbial thick and thin. In all likelihood, neither would ever have a better friend. But at no point had either of them ever forgotten their respective stations. Now the valet felt it might be imprudent to confess that he was responsible for the major's pursuit of Lady Harriet. He'd counted on her good sense to handle the matter. But it appeared that his scheme had gone awry. Well if the worst came to the worst, he'd simply have to have a word with the lady and take the consequences.

"He's a handsome devil, ain't he, Shaftoe?"

"The major?" The valet wrinkled his nose. "I suppose so. If you care for the Adonis type."

"Too pretty by half for my tastes, too. But he's precisely the type females seem to go for."

"Come now, Colonel. I've never known you to be so blue-deviled. Why, he can't hold a candle to you, sir. There's nobody can match your success with the fair sex."

"Success you call it?" the other growled as he started for the door. "Botched the only business I ever gave a tinker's damn for."

"Whoosh!" Shaftoe breathed as the door closed. He'd never seen his employer's confidence so low. He was beginning to feel the pangs of remorse, but then, as he tidied up the dressing table, his sense of humor took over from his conscience and he began to chuckle. Colonel Sir Rawdon Melford was a prince of a fellow, true enough. Still, a little humbling wouldn't do the toff a bit of harm. The valet resumed his cheerful whistling.

The fact that the colonel encountered Lady Harriet in the hallway did nothing to alleviate his rotten mood. He looked her up and down, from the top of her flaming hair, crowned with a wreath of small white rosebuds, to her jade silk ball gown and her satin slippers. "Well, you're looking magnificent, I see." His voice was funereal.

"Thank you. I think."

"That's the gown you wore at our betrothal ball, isn't it?"

"Well, yes. But I must say since that was donkey's years ago it's most untactful of you to recall it."

"How could I forget? When you were coming at me like one of the Furies, I thought you were the most gorgeous female I'd ever seen."

"If you thought that," she sniffed, "you've got your analogies a bit confused. As I recall, the Furies were perfect horrors."

"Well, you always were the scholar of us two." He was staring at her bare neck and shoulders. "But didn't you wear an emerald necklace with that?"

"Yes, as a matter of fact. And before you're rude enough to ask, I sold it. And, no, I could not afford to have a paste copy made even if I'd wanted to, which I didn't." They were walking down the stairs.

"You should have kept the diamonds I gave you. I told you to."

"Well I could hardly break our engagement and keep your betrothal gift, now could I?"

"I don't see why not. No need to stand on points with me."

"I'll wager," she pointedly changed the subject, "that you didn't have *your* evening clothes eight years ago."

"Are you implying that I couldn't still get into 'em? I'll have you know I weigh exactly the same. Or near enough."

She laughed up at him. "Have I pricked your vanity, Rawdon? You always were long on that. No, I simply meant that you look, as usual, up to the latest crack. Still very much the dandy. Did Weston make that coat?"

"And speaking of dandies," he muttered as they entered the crowded ballroom and spotted Major Mortram making his way toward them. "You two must look like a brushfire when you put your heads together." The myriad candles in the enormous chandeliers highlighted the major's ruddy locks.

If the major's evening clothes lacked the perfection of the colonel's, he atoned for this shortcoming by the magnificence of his smile. "Ah, there you are, Lady Harriet. The first dance is mine, I believe."

"I'm afraid you mistake the matter, sir. Lady Harriet will be standing up with me."

There was something in the colonel's countenance that persuaded the major not to contest the point. Even Lady Harriet choked down her protest when she took a closer look at his granite face.

But after Major Mortram had bowed himself away, she turned on her escort angrily. "That was certainly ragmannered. What on earth's come over you?"

"The first dance is a waltz," he answered simply. "And do you realize that we've never once waltzed together? It was considered shocking back when we were—friends."

Yes, and we should have left it that way, was her first thought when he took her in his arms and an electric shock ran through her body. No wonder they used to frown on this.

He was a superb dancer. Plenty of practice, Harriet reminded herself just before surrendering to the music and the moment. She had meant to show him she was as skilled as he was, but that bit of prideful competition was soon forgotten. The waltz was magic. He was the perfect partner. There was no past, no thought of the future. There was only the music and the candlelight that sparkled from every dangling crystal prism and every gilded mirror. Her feet were winged. They never came in contact with the parquet floor. His eyes, intense and blue, held hers. She refused to read them.

The couple was totally unaware of the striking picture they presented as they whirled around the floor—the tall, willowy beauty whose jade-green gown turned her hair to flame, the handsome man, a full head taller, whose bearing gave him a military distinction civilian clothing could not conceal. Though oblivious to it, they were the center of everyone's attention, while those who knew their history gasped and hastened to pass their story along to the few who didn't.

When the last strains of the violins had ended, neither waltzer had a word to spare for the other. Lady Harriet's next partner was waiting to claim her hand. The colonel bowed formally and went striding from the room.

# Chapter
# Twenty-one

Miss susan tunstall had been one of those watching the former sweethearts. But not for the same reason as the others in the room. She had arrived too late to be engaged for the first dance and stood near the entryway, half-concealed behind a bower of roses.

Her interest in the couple was entirely personal. She was regretting that she had estranged herself from the colonel and remembering how she'd adored the tall, distinguished charmer when she was a child and he'd tossed her in the air and galloped with her on his shoulders. She was working up her courage to ask his advice. But then he'd gone striding past without ever seeing her, and the moment passed.

Major Brent Mortram had watched the waltzers in a towering rage. He berated himself for allowing the arrogant baronet to outface him. He did not miss a single nuance of the charged sexuality of the dance, of the way the couple moved together in perfect rhythm, of how their gazes locked.

Mortram was plunged into the greatest conflict of his life. And like the gambler he was, he'd come prepared to hedge his bets. If given no other choice, he planned to elope with Susan Tunstall. He'd just enough blunt, he'd calculated, to take them to Gretna Green. (Thank God, he'd been able to fob off Flack's hints about paying his shot at the Magpie.) But how they'd manage for all those years till the little widgeon came into her inheritance, God only knew. Of course she did possess some jewels he could sell to stake him in some games of chance. Then, too, once the deed was done and Susan was irrevocably his wife, perhaps her mother and stepfather would come around. Mortram was, by necessity of his trade, prone to look on the bright side of things.

So what he hoped for most was that he'd not be forced to elope with Miss Susan Tunstall. For he'd come very close to falling in love with Lady Harriet. But aside from such personal feelings, which experience had taught him were subject to change, was this overriding consideration: There'd be very little waiting around for that fortune.

True, Lady Harriet would not be pliable like Susan Tunstall. There was no doubt but that her ladyship possessed a strong mind of her own. But he quite looked forward to the process of taming her. It was a bad beginning, though, to have let that haughty, gentry cove steal her out from under his very nose. Luckily he had engaged her ladyship for two other dances. That should give him ample time to make his move.

"Psst! Major!" Mortram jumped as a voice spoke from a bank of flowers behind him. "We must talk."

Oh God, it's starting. The major got a grip upon himself and turned to focus a gleaming smile of welcome upon Lady Selina.

\* \* \*

184

"You've hardly said a word all evening."

Evelyn Forbes had extracted Miss Tunstall from among the flowery decorations and persuaded her to stand up with him. But he was frowning with concern. What had happened to the vivacious young lady who had so enjoyed the Maying the day before? Now she might well be facing her execution. "Look here, Susan, is something wrong?" he blurted.

"Why no, of course not."

"Dammit, don't try and gammon me. Are you sickening for something? You're pale as a ghost, and you're practically wasting away. I'll vow you were a full stone heavier when I first saw you."

"Well if I've lost a bit of weight, at least that's one thing to the good." She forced a smile.

"I don't happen to agree. I thought you looked—just splendid."

"You did?"

At that point they were swept up into the dance.

At the end of the cotillion, Lady Selina was waiting for them. "Susan, may I have a word with you?" Evelyn watched with narrowed eyes as the twosome left the ballroom. Without knowing why he thought so, he was certain that Miss Tunstall did not desire the tête-à-tête.

"I've talked to him. Everything's ready." Selina's eyes were shining as she shut the bedchamber door behind them. She loved an adventure, even secondhand. And her enthusiasm was far too great to be dampened down by her friend's apparent lack of that commodity. "Everything will be marvelous, you'll see," she said encouragingly as the two shared the dressing table bench, making unnecessary adjustments to their coiffures. "There's absolutely nothing

185

to be afraid of. From here on out the major will take care of you." She waited for a response, and Susan managed a wan smile. Quite willing to take even such a feeble effort as an expression of agreement, Selina moved on to the logistics of elopement. "Did you pack a portmanteau? Good." She beamed her approval of this much cooperation on the other's part. "Major Mortram says you're to slip out after supper and meet him at the west front carriage drive. I thought myself that you should leave earlier to get a head start in case anyone misses you at bedtime and gives chase. But he says you'll need sustenance to drive all night, and I expect he's right. Come on." She stood abruptly and pulled her craven comrade by the hand. "We'd best get back to the ball before anyone suspects something's afoot."

Evelyn was impatiently waiting to partner Selina for a country dance. He looked at her suspiciously as they took their places. "You're up to something, aren't you?" he whispered.

"I'm sure I've no notion of what you mean."

"Don't play the innocent with me. You've got that cat-caught-in-the-cream look, and I know to my sorrow what that means. What did you want with Susan just now?"

"*Susan*? Aren't you being overly familiar, *Mr.* Forbes? She's 'Miss Tunstall' to you, I'd think." Suddenly her eyes widened as a thought struck. "You aren't in love with her, are you, Evelyn?" He reddened. "Oh my goodness, you are!" she exclaimed.

"For God's sake, keep your voice down."

"Oh but Evelyn, you can't be." Selina felt a surge of pity for her oldest friend. "Susan's not for you."

"And just why not?" he bristled.

"Oh, it's nothing personal." She lowered her voice, melodramatically. "It's just that you're too late. Her heart belongs to another."

"The devil it does. Oh I know she fancies herself in love with that here and therein." He shot a darkling look in the direction of another set, where the major was gazing soulfully into Lady Harriet's eyes. "But it's obvious the fellow's fallen for Lady Harriet. He's making a cake of himself over her."

Selina's expression was one-half pity, one-half scorn. "The major's not interested in Lady Harriet. He's merely diverting attention away from Susan so that no one will suspect that—" Her voice trailed off as she realized she'd gone too far.

"So no one will suspect what?" he pounced.

But at that moment they were separated, and when at last the dance reunited them, he was not able to persuade her to say more.

It was with relief that Selina gave her hand to Soame Townshend at the conclusion of that dance. She had come uncomfortably close to letting the cat out of the bag and was berating herself for being such a rattle. She did hope that Soame wasn't also suspicious. She couldn't bear another inquisition.

But that young man had other things than Susan and the major on his mind. "I could hardly wait to tell you," he confided as they took their places. "You know that position I applied for, secretary to the ambassador? Well I just heard. I've got it. I'll be leaving for Vienna right away."

Selina felt her heart, unexpectedly, plummet. But she rallied all her resources and forced a smile. "Oh congratulations, Mr. Townshend. That is marvelous news. And how I envy you. Living in Vienna! What an adventure you'll be having."

"I know. I can hardly believe my good fortune." He gave her a sudden whirl, uncalled for by the figure of the dance.

"Do you know what I've been thinking ever since I learned of my appointment?" he asked when their heads began to clear. "You must come to Vienna for a long visit. The ambassador's wife is a particular friend of mine. In fact," he grinned, "I shouldn't be surprised if that's not how I got the appointment. I'll ask her to invite you."

"Oh would you? That would be famous! Only," her face fell once more, "I'm not sure Papa will give his permission."

"Of course he will. I'll get Mariana to ask him. Do you seriously believe he'll refuse her anything?" And their eyes traveled to where Lord and Lady Fawcett were seated near the orchestra. Their heads were close together, and they were holding hands—very bad ton indeed.

"You're right, of course. Oh what a marvelous stroke of luck it was when Papa fell in love with your sister!"

After his hurried conversation with Selina, Major Mortram had waited impatiently to stand up with Lady Harriet. As they took their places in the set, he tried to mask the desperation he felt by turning all his considerable charm, full force, upon this lady. But he was uncomfortably conscious of the fact that Melford had come back into the ballroom. The colonel was lounging against the wall, arms folded, staring their way.

"My dear, dear Lady Harriet," Mortram whispered in her ear after they'd been separated and rejoined by the music. "I must speak privately with you or else go mad. Do say you'll stroll in the garden with me in place of our next dance."

"Really, Major Mortram, I don't think—" Then she, too, became aware that Rawdon Melford was glowering their way. She smiled to herself and changed her mind. "Very well then, Major. But only for a moment, you understand."

At the conclusion of the set, Evelyn Forbes practically pounced as Harriet and the major left the floor.

"I believe we have the next dance, Lady Harriet."

"Well, actually, I think you mistake the matter," she'd begun after Major Mortram had left them, "I'm promised to the squire."

"I know, but I simply must talk to you. Privately. It's fearfully important."

One look at his face cut off her protest. She took his arm and tried to ignore Rawdon's curious stare as they passed near him on their way out of the ballroom.

The library was deserted when they entered. "Now what's this all about?" she asked as they sat down on a settee by an open window. A welcome breeze was stirring the curtains.

He came bluntly to the point. "Just what do you know about that Mortram fellow?"

"Why very little really, except that he was in the army and is touring about the country. And that he's quite charming and amusing."

"Too charming and amusing by half, if you ask me. Tell me, Lady Harriet, just why the devil would a man like that be courting you?"

She laughed as he realized what he'd just said and blushed furiously.

"Oh my God, what a clod you must think me. Believe me, I did not mean—"

"Of course you did. But all insults aside, I can tell you're quite serious, so I'll be. And I'll confess that I've asked myself the very same question. He's certainly not dangling after my fortune," she observed dryly. "We can rule that out."

He tried to proceed a bit more delicately this time. "You haven't by chance—uh—fallen in love with him, have you?"

"No, I have not."

"Well, that's a big relief. For you see, according to Selina, the blackguard's simply using you. To cover up the fact he's followed Susan Tunstall here. And, frankly, I think the man's an out-and-out fortune hunter. And from the hints Selina's dropped, I fear they're planning an elopement. Somehow we've got to stop them." He sounded desperate.

"Calm down a bit, Evelyn, and tell me, slowly, what this is all about."

After he'd disclosed the whole story of Susan's odd behavior, Selina's hints, and the ubiquitous major's presence in the places where Susan and Selina were most apt to ride, Harriet sat a moment in deep thought. Then she suddenly had an inspiration.

"If you're right, and I expect you are, especially that our major has an ulterior motive for pursuing me, well, all we have to do is disillusion your Susan. Am I not right?"

He reddened. "She's not *my* Susan, but, yes, that's just what's needed. The thing is, I'm convinced that we haven't much time."

"Well, disillusionment doesn't take much time, believe me." There was a touch of bitterness in her voice. "I think I know just the thing. Listen, here's what you must do."

Sometime later, as the orchestra struck up the music for a boulanger, there was a general exodus from the ballroom. Lord and Lady Fawcett were the first to slip away and enjoy the fragrance of the garden, and the soft light of the full moon that would provide their guests a safe journey home.

Moments after, Evelyn Forbes claimed Susan Tunstall's hand for their second dance together. He was alarmed to see how ill she was looking. "I do have the headache," she admitted under his probing.

"Then what you need is fresh air." She made no protest when he took her arm and guided her outside.

Major Mortram did not see them go. His concern was all for Lady Harriet. He feared she might change her mind about the stroll that he'd suggested. But when he claimed her hand for the dance that he'd been promised, she was quite eager for a walk. This state of affairs boded well, he concluded, for a satisfactory outcome to his suit.

Colonel Melford's glinting eyes were focused on the handsome couple as they hurried through the glass doors that opened onto a balustraded terrace. He gave them a minute's head start and then followed.

The grounds sloped gently down from the terrace in an open vista that carried the eye toward a serpentine pond, glistening with moonlight. At one end of the pond was a false bridge that served as part dam and part overlook. This focal point became everyone's destination. But only the major and Lady Harriet took the most direct approach.

When Harriet had suggested that they visit the bridge, the major would have preferred a less conspicuous route. But since he was unaware of the alternate paths that led through the wooded sections on either side, he made no demur. Evelyn and Susan had taken one of these a bit before. Colonel Melford, making sure he was unobserved, chose the other.

Lord Fawcett, who had taken his wife away from the party for the sole purpose of making love to her, was well aware of the bridge's conspicuous position and had spent very little time upon it. Instead, he had guided Mariana behind a backdrop of rhododendron and was kissing her passionately when they heard voices. "Let's stay very still," he murmured in her ear. "Maybe they'll soon go away."

Lady Harriet was lecturing Major Mortram on the influence that the great landscape artist, Capability Brown, had had on Lord Fawcett's park. The major, conscious that time was running out for him, listened impatiently. He felt rather like exclaiming, "Blast Capability Brown!" He would not have dreamed that Lady Harriet could become a worse rattle than Lady Selina Fawcett, but there it was. He was wondering just how he was going to shut her up and propose marriage, when all of a sudden she ceased, mid-description, on her own accord.

For Harriet, who had maneuvered them to the exact center of the bridge, had at last seen the signal she'd been waiting for. Evelyn Forbes, now lurking on the edge of the west wood, was vigorously waving a handkerchief over Susan Tunstall's unsuspecting head.

As the white linen flashed wildly back and forth, Harriet didn't hesitate. She rose on tiptoe, placed her hands against the major's lapels, and raised her lips to his. Not a man prone to caviling in the face of his own good fortune, Mortram crushed her to his chest and kissed her.

"Now who do you suppose that is?"

Evelyn strove to sound offhand as he directed his companion's attention to the bridge. Then, as Susan gasped and stiffened, he pushed his dubious playacting ability one step further. "By George!" he exclaimed. "Why, I do believe it's Lady Harriet and that Major Mortram. I'd no idea the wind was blowing in that direction, had you, Susan?"

Miss Tunstall didn't answer. She had wheeled and was hurrying back up the tree-lined path while tears of rage—and relief—gathered in her eyes.

Colonel Sir Rawdon Melford, baronet, was also spurred into instant action. But retreat was not in the colonel's nature. He had watched the attractive twosome stroll to the center of the bridge. He had seen his beloved raise her lips invitingly toward the major's. And at the very moment when the delighted major had accepted the invitation, he had started sprinting swiftly and silently on his soft-soled dancing shoes.

Lady Harriet felt it necessary to prolong the kiss, to make sure the silly Tunstall child had had time to see it. But she was finding it tedious in the extreme. And somewhere in the recesses of her mind, she recorded a slight twinge of disappointment. She had expected more fireworks from the attractive major. Then, just as she was wondering if she couldn't now at last give the gentleman a parting shove, all initiative was taken from her. Rawdon Melford had come bounding across the mock bridge uttering a throaty growl. He jerked Lady Harriet out of Mortram's arms, and planted a facer on the lover, which sent him reeling backward against the bridge rail. Not one to ignore so strategic an opportunity, the colonel then grabbed the stunned gentleman by the legs and hoisted him over the balustrade. He landed with a resounding, showering splash.

"Rawdon!" Lady Harriet shrieked. "Have you gone stark mad? You'll drown him."

"In five feet of water? I think not, more's the pity. But if you're so concerned, here, you go save him." And with that he picked up her ladyship and tossed her, too, among the lily pads. Then, satisfied with his evening's work, the colonel dusted off his white-gloved palms and went striding from the bridge.

"My God, they're at it again!" Lord Fawcett's horrified voice floated out of the rhododendron. "Can't imagine what it is about balls and pools of water that seems to set 'em off. But didn't I warn you, m'dear, that it was a real mistake to invite those two hotheads here together?"

# Chapter
# Twenty-two

It WAS NOON before Colonel Melford dragged himself, groaning, out of bed. He was suffering the devil's own pounding head, the result of an inordinate consumption of brandy. As memory came flooding back, he groaned still louder. "Pack up my things, Shaftoe," he said thickly, as he took the steaming cup of tea from the valet's hand. "I'm leaving." He took a reviving sip. "Oh, no need to look so Friday-faced. You'll stay in Mitford, of course."

A little later there was an emotional farewell between master and man, as the one prepared to leave for London and the other for the Magpie. "Work out the best deal you can get from the old skinflint," the colonel admonished, "and let me know what the tab is."

"You'll come to the wedding, sir?"

"Wouldn't miss it." The colonel tried to force himself to look happy for his boyhood comrade. It wasn't easy.

After a formal farewell to his host and hostess, made more difficult by Lord Fawcett's tendency to grin, Rawdon climbed into his curricle. He was in the very act of flourishing his whip when his arm halted. "Where's that damn dog?" he muttered.

A search of the stables, accompanied by ear-splitting whistles that did little for his throbbing head, produced nothing. "Well, at least it's on my way," he consoled himself.

Sure enough, as he clattered up the cobblestone street in front of Harriet's cottage, Adolphus came bounding out to greet him, accompanied by the faithful Christobel. But when the colonel tried to whistle the dog up beside him in the curricle, the mongrel turned coy and ran to the backgarden with the greyhound bitch. There his cursing master managed to grab a fistful of the nape of his neck and drag him, whimpering, out of the hollyhocks. "Come on, you cur, you're not wanted around here."

"You're rather late with that perception, Rawdon," a dry voice spoke behind him. "Christobel's *enceinte*." He released his hold and spun around to face Lady Harriet.

"What the devil are you doing here?"

"I live here, remember? When I saw your rig I actually supposed you'd come to find out whether or not you drowned me. But now I see you only wished to claim that mutt."

"You're damn right I didn't come to see you. I thought you'd be halfway to Gretna Green by now."

Her eyebrows rose. "Why would you think a daft thing like that?"

"Oh come down off your high boughs, Harry. I didn't get so drunk last night that I forgot you kissed that fellow. My God, woman, you actually threw yourself into his arms like some lewd, bawdy-house queen."

"Watch it, Rawdon." Her eyes narrowed. "You

haven't the slightest notion of what went on there. And speaking of throwing—you might have drowned me, you know."

"Damned unlikely. You swim like a fish."

"Well, you certain left poor Major Mortram the worse for wear." She struggled to keep her face straight. "His swollen nose does nothing for his beauty."

"Good. And if you're thinking of marrying that here and therein, you'd better know he's not a major. Never been in the army, so Shaftoe discovered. Nothing but a Jack Sharp, pure and simple."

"Well that's hardly a surprise."

"You mean you don't care? God, woman, you disgust me. I thought you had more sense, Harry, than to fall for an Adonis profile."

"I don't see why you'd think a thing like that." She reached up and turned his head sideways. "I certainly made a fool of myself over your profile in my salad days."

He removed her hand, but almost against his will held on to it. "I resent the comparison," he growled.

"Well, you should not, for you and Major—you and *Mister* Mortram have a great deal in common. You're both in the business of female conquest. You, of course, have a fortune to help you along, whereas he has to rely solely on his looks and wits. Which makes him rather the more admirable, wouldn't you say?"

"You're really enjoying twisting the knife, aren't you, Harry?" He dropped her hand and they stood toe-to-toe, glaring at each other, while their dogs looked at them curiously. "So come on. Out with it. What do you intend to do about the fellow?"

"Do? Why nothing. It's all been done. Though you

came within an ace of spoiling everything when you came charging across the bridge that way. But then, of course, I expect your assault had very little to do with what was actually going on."

"It had everything to do with what was going on. I tell you, I really saw red. You know," he paused reflectively, "I always thought that was just a daft expression, but red's actually what I saw. But never mind that. I went a bit crazy when I saw you throw yourself at that scoundrel's head."

"Oh indeed?" she said quietly. "Then I expect you now know how I felt eight years ago."

"That comparison won't hold up, Harry. There was a good explanation for what happened then. But with your fiery temper you never gave me a chance to make it. Then, by God, you'd cried off in the papers before I even knew what hit me."

"Let's just say that your past finally caught up with you, Rawdon. The opera dancers. Mrs. Fowles. All the rest of them."

"I know I wasn't a saint. But I did love you, you know. I just thought it was all right to sow some wild oats before I settled down. Now I can see that I mistook the matter."

"Well, it was a bit much to keep on sowing them at our engagement party. You'll surely admit that."

"I'll admit no such thing. Damn it, Harry, that woman kissed *me*. In exactly the same way you flung yourself in the arms of that underbred Casanova—which was supposed to be the point of this discussion, if you recall."

"Well, I'm sure you relished your revenge for the public humiliation I'd caused you."

"Not really. If that had been my intention, I'd have

collected a crowd the way you did. Lord and Lady Fawcett hardly comprise an audience."

"Oh, but your ward and Evelyn Forbes were witnesses as well. That was what the whole thing was supposed to be about, you clodpole. And you almost ruined it." Harriet then went on to tell him of the impending elopement and the plot she'd hatched to disillusion Susan Tunstall.

"But I don't understand." Rawdon shook his head to clear it. "If Mortram planned to hare off to Scotland with an heiress, why was he risking it all that way? No, don't tell me. I understand. Undoubtedly the poor sapskull fell in love with you."

There was a long pause while Lady Harriet struggled with her conscience. "Oh blast! As much as I'd enjoy letting you believe that, the truth is, Shaftoe told him I was coming into a great deal of money right away, and that Susan wouldn't get hers till she was twenty-five."

"The devil he did!"

"He realized what was happening, don't you see, and thought this was a good way to prevent the elopement. He felt sure I could handle the major."

"And could you?"

"Oh yes indeed. I thoroughly enjoyed being pursued. Though I will admit it was a bit lowering to find out it was my fortune that attracted him and not all my sterling qualities. But then, that's the way of the world. And my vanity's a small price to pay to save Miss Tunstall. I expect she'll wish to marry Evelyn now. Do you think your cousin will approve?"

"The devil take Miss Tunstall!" he flared. "You might have told me what was going on, Harry. But then I expect you liked to see me squirm."

"I would have done, I collect, if I had dreamed that it was possible." She looked up at him quizzically. "Were you actually jealous, Rawdon?"

"Damn right I was. And I never suspected any ulterior motive on Mortram's part. And I still doubt that the poor fool was that good an actor. No, it's not wonderful to me that any cove would love you for yourself. I always have, you know."

"No, I didn't know. But then Shaftoe said so."

"The devil he did. When?"

"When I came dripping up to my room last night. We had quite an illuminating coze. Among other things, he kept insisting that you've always loved me. And of course I have the greatest respect for Jem Shaftoe's perceptions. I expect he knows you far better than you know yourself."

"Well then it's a great pity I didn't send him around eight years ago," he said sarcastically.

"Oh I doubt it would have worked. I had far too much pride then."

"And now?"

"Try me."

"Lady Harriet," he recited, mock seriously, "will you do me the honor of becoming my wife?"

"Yes."

His jaw dropped. "Just like that?"

"Well, no, not entirely. Let's see now. How did that 'lewd bawdy-house queen' business go?" She stood on tiptoe and her raised lips found his. His cooperation was speedy, fiercely passionate, and prolonged while both dogs chased back and forth, barking wildly.

"Well," he murmured into her hair once the kiss had ended and her face was buried in his chest, "at least we'll prove that old hag of a gypsy wrong."

"How's that?" she asked, looking up at him.

"She said you were to wed a tall, handsome, red-haired stranger. Mortram, in other words."

"Well, no, not actually," she confessed. "I just made that up to sound mysterious. What she did predict was that I'd marry someone from my past who was"—she ticked the qualities off on her fingers—"tall, handsome, brilliant, dashing, charming, witty, wealthy."

"Did she, by George?" He tried to look amazed. "Well, now, that's uncanny, that is. Creepy, you might almost say. She may have messed up on some of her predictions, but the old crone certainly hit this one square on the mark."

"Square on the mark? Never. I'd say, personally, that the gypsy missed it by a mile. Due to being overcoached, most likely. Still, who am I to quibble? A tall, rich, old acquaintance is close enough."

She laughed at his expression, then reached up and drew his head down. "Could we try that 'lewd bawdy-house queen' maneuver once again?" she murmured.

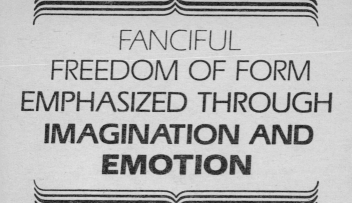

# FANCIFUL FREEDOM OF FORM EMPHASIZED THROUGH IMAGINATION AND EMOTION

# Marian Devon